THE SIEGE OF THE SUPERS

LOGAN RUTHERFORD

Cover Art by Damonza (www.damonza.com)
Copyedited and Proofread by Carol Davis (www.caroldavisauthor.com)
Additional Proofreading by Donna Rich
Fragments & Fictions

Part I:

The Return of Tempest

Chapter 1
The Man at the Door

September 20th, 2078

AGENT CASSIDY OPENED the front door to the Tempest Memorial Museum and saw Leopold Renner standing there, clutching at the bloody bullet wounds in his torso.

"Leopold!" she breathed as she bent down to catch the man as he slumped to the ground. She brought a finger up to her earpiece. "Mayday, mayday. This is Agent Cassidy speaking. Epsilon is down. I repeat, Epsilon is down. Requesting extraction immediately."

Agent Cassidy dragged Leopold into the foyer of the museum, shutting the door behind her. She locked it, then returned to Leopold's side. His heavy, wet breathing struck panic into Cassidy with every breath. She put pressure on the wounds, doing her best to stop the bleeding.

Leopold grabbed Cassidy with a bloody hand. She looked into his crazed eyes, unsure of what more to do. She was trained on how to take a life, not save one. She didn't have the tools necessary to keep him alive. All she could do was hope extraction would come soon. She clicked her earpiece again. "I repeat, mayday, immediate extraction requisition. Epsilon is do—"

"Y-y-you're n-not Mrs. Andr—"

"—Leopold, stop speaking. We're gonna get you out of this, okay?" Cassidy said.

Leopold nodded his head. His eyes focused on the ceiling as he concentrated on his breathing.

"Hello?" Cassidy screamed into her earpiece. "Epsilon is *dying* here!"

"Agent Cassidy?" a voice said.

Her heart fluttered. "Damien?"

"Yes. Omaha Delta Foxtrot nine five."

"Charlie Alpha Omaha five two."

"Identity confirmed. Cassidy, we're under attack up here. We're trying to get to you as fast as we can. Whatever you do, keep Epsilon alive. We're doing what we can on our end. We're trying to get to you as fast as we can, but we're taking heavy fire."

"Damien, I don't know how much ti—"

"—Cassidy I have to g*—oh, shit!*"

An explosion came through the radio. "*Damien!*" Cassidy screamed.

"Cassidy! Get out of there!"

The line went dead.

"Damien? Damien?" Cassidy spoke into the earpiece. Nothing but silence.

"When are you all going to learn that I *hate* red? It just doesn't look good on me," a familiar voice spoke from across the room.

Agent Cassidy looked up. Standing in front of the crimson Tempest headpiece stood the man himself. Nineteen-year-old Kane Andrews turned and faced her.

"Hey there, Cass," he said with a sly smile. He was wearing a red t-shirt under a tan leather jacket, and a dark pair of jeans. Very different from what she usually saw him in—his Tempest outfit.

Cassidy stood, and instinctively thrust her arm out to her side, activating her powers. But the purple lighting didn't course across her arms like it usually did. In fact, nothing at all happened.

Kane chuckled. "Aw, that was kinda pathetic."

Cassidy cursed herself silently for looking like a fool in front of Kane. "What do you want, Kane?"

Kane took a step forward. "I'm taking Leopold. Stand aside, Cassidy. I don't want to have to fight you."

Cassidy planted her feet in front of Leopold. "You're not taking him anywhere. Epsilon is property of the UHA."

Kane continued walking forward, still confident. "Help isn't coming, Cassidy. My people are keeping yours occupied. You know very well what we're capable of."

"You know very well what *I'm* capable of, Kane," Cassidy said.

"I know very well," Kane said with a smile.

She thought back to the last time they'd fought. It hadn't ended well for Kane, and he clearly remembered that.

"But your powers don't work here, Cassidy."

"Neither do yours. We're even." She moved into a fighting stance. "You're not taking Epsilon."

Kane sighed. "So that's how it's going to be?"

Cassidy said nothing.

"Very well."

She lunged at Kane before he was ready, and planted her fist in his cheek. He stumbled back, but put his hands up to block her next punch.

Now he was ready, and their fight began.

Chapter 2
Crash Landing

January 24th, 2016

MY EYES CRACKED open as I inhaled a deep breath.

"Oh, shit, he's awake!" I heard someone shout into their radio over the loud roar of an engine.

"Hit 'em with neutralizer! I'm almost at the landing strip!"

My eyes shot open. Facing me were two people wearing uniforms with NASA insignia badges on the chest.

Time slowed as an arc of purple electricity came right for my chest. My instincts took over.

I shot straight back, the purple electricity barely missing me, and slammed into the rear of the aircraft. The back half of the plane flew off when I impacted, and I shot out into the night sky.

I went tumbling through the air, dodging objects that were being sucked out of the hole in the plane. I could see the people inside holding on for dear life as I righted myself in the air, gaining my composure.

"We're going down!" the pilot shouted.

The plane began spiraling toward the ground. The plane

had a weird shape to it… and that's when I realized it wasn't a plane. It was a space shuttle.

I watched it as it continued to fall. My mind was hazy, and my body ached. I looked at my surroundings, and couldn't see a thing. It was pitch black, and the farther away the crashing space shuttle fell, the more quiet it got.

Soon, the only sound I could hear was my own breathing. I hovered in the air, trying to put together the pieces. Trying to figure out what was going on.

The screams of the people in the shuttle reached my ears, jolting me into action.

I'm Kane Andrews. I'm Tempest. I'm a superhero. And even though I wasn't sure what was going on, I had a job to do.

I flew toward the space shuttle as it spiraled toward the ground. There was a pop behind me as I broke the sound barrier, traveling faster and faster toward my target.

The shuttle lit up the night sky, flames shooting out from the hole I'd created. I flew toward it at super speed, the wind whipping past, filling me with life. Everything was becoming clearer and clearer.

I slowed as I reached the shuttle. I flew through the back of it and grabbed the two people who had been sitting next to the bed they'd had me strapped into.

I flew back out, the flames from the shuttle licking my skin. The people I held—a man and a woman—screamed as I flew toward the ground. I flew fast, as I was going to have to go back up to the shuttle and get the remaining astronauts, and the shuttle was getting closer and closer to the ground.

I hit the ground as softly and gracefully as I could, and set the two people down in a large wheat field. I jumped up, flying right back into action.

In the time it took me to save the first two people, the shuttle had increased the speed of its descent, and it was now just a few hundred feet from slamming into the ground.

I flew as fast as I could, the stalks of wheat in the field below blown back as I hit supersonic speed not far from the ground.

The shuttle was hundreds of yards away, but I reached it in a matter of seconds. I flew in and grabbed the pilot and co-pilot from their seats as they struggled to gain control of the shuttle.

We were just a few stories above the ground, seconds away from slamming into it and turning into a huge fireball.

I flew out of the shuttle, moving away from it as fast as I could—but I was unable to reach top speed since my passengers wouldn't be able to handle it.

I turned my back to the shuttle and did the best I could to shield the pilots with my body.

The shuttle hit the ground in a massive explosion. My supersensitive eardrums ruptured with a pop, and blood trickled from them. I felt my body immediately get to work repairing them. The flames licked at my back, followed closely by black smoke.

I continued to fly away toward the field. I found where I'd dropped off the first two astronauts and dropped their pilots off with them. They were radioing for help when I returned. They all looked at me, dumbfounded and afraid.

"Is help coming for you?" I asked, shaking my vocal cords to disguise my voice.

The female astronaut nodded as she pointed at the radio on her belt.

I wanted to say something more, like a one-liner or

something. But I didn't have the energy. My mind still felt hazy, and my body ached. All I wanted was to clear my mind.

I turned away from the four astronauts, leaving them in the wheat field. I flew over the flaming wreckage of the space shuttle, and toward the most peaceful place I knew.

That place was Ebon, Indiana. Home.

*

I scanned the area around my home outside of Ebon. There was no sign of any government agents or surveillance. Relief washed through me. They hadn't figured out my identity. Any DNA samples they'd taken from me en route from the Moon to Earth had been destroyed in the crash, which meant when it came to figuring out who Tempest was, they were still at square one. At least, that's what I told myself. They surely had pictures of my face, and those images had to have been transmitted back to NASA. Still, there was no one around my home, so I was safe for now.

I flew down softly and slowly to the back door of our two-story house. I twisted the doorknob, but it wouldn't budge. I ran around to the front door and tried opening it, but it was locked as well.

I sighed as I knocked on the door. This would be the one time my parents wouldn't be mad at me for returning home in the middle of the night.

I heard movement on the other side of the door. My heart beat faster and faster. Even though to me it seemed like no time had passed, I felt a longing for my parents hit me like a punch from Richter. The last time I'd seen them had been before my big battle, and I wanted nothing more than to see them again. I could only imagine how they felt after not seeing me for—I realized I didn't even know how long I'd been gone. What if I'd been gone for a long time? Like, years? How much would my parents have changed? What if they'd forgotten about me?

Anxiety replaced my longing. I cursed under my breath at Dad for taking so long to answer the door.

The knob twisted, and the door opened.

My heart skipped a beat. Heat rushed to my head. I thought I was about to pass out.

"You're not my dad."

Chapter 3
Homecoming

I LOOKED INTO THE eyes of the old man standing at the door of my home.

"Who the hell are you?" he asked in a tired tone. The wisps of grey hair on his head were frizzy and disheveled. He stared at me with angry, tired eyes.

"Who the hell are *you*? Where's Andy Andrews?" I asked, my throat drying. I felt dizzy and sick. I looked around behind the old man, searching for any sign of my parents. From what I could see, the walls had been repainted a cream color, not the maroon I was used to.

"Andy hasn't lived here for months," the man said. He was becoming more and more lucid, which meant he was more and more angry and perturbed. "I don't know who you think you are, or who you think I am, but you'd best get out of here before I call the cops."

I was bewildered. At a loss for words, I began to back up.

"Hey, wait a second. What's that you got on?" the old man asked.

I looked down. Even though it was tattered, torn, and

faded, you could clearly tell it was my Tempest outfit. I didn't know what to do.

The gears began to turn in the man's head as he began to put the pieces together.

"This isn't—I'm not—" I began.

"Frank? Who is it, Frank?" I heard the voice of an elderly woman say in the background. I looked behind Frank and saw a short old woman peering around the corner at the end of the foyer. Her hair was pinned up and she was wearing a pink silk nightgown that she clutched in fear.

Her eyes went wide when she saw me standing there. I could hear her heartbeat skip and then speed up. I could see her knuckles whiten as she gripped her nightgown with all her might, even from where I was standing outside the front door.

"This isn't what it looks like," I said.

Frank looked me up and down. "I saw you in pictures when we toured the place. You're Andy's kid. You're Temp—"

The old man's eyes lit up, and he stumbled. I ran to his side and caught him before he could hit the ground, and brought him down gently.

"What are you doing?" the old lady screamed. "What are you doing to my hu—"

The same thing happened to her, and I ran across the room, catching her too.

"What's going on?" I said. The old man and woman were lying on the ground, their eyes glowing, breathing heavily.

The light in both their eyes faded, and the glowing stopped. Their eyes closed, and I could hear them breathing softly.

"Uh, hello? Can you hear me?" a familiar female voice said in my head.

Samantha? I thought.

"I'm gonna assume you're trying to think what you're saying. Yeah, you're going to have to talk out loud. I can't read your mind. I can just see, smell, feel, and hear everything you can."

"Can you tell me what's going on with this couple?" I asked frantically. "Something's wrong, I don't know what to do."

"Just relax. I'm wiping the last few minutes of their memories. Let me tell you, that's *really* hard to do. My head is pounding, so I'll be leaving your mind now. Just get to the Los Angeles Self Storage by the UCLA campus. I'm in storage unit 306. I'll try to explain what I can when you get here."

I nodded my head. Then I realized that she probably couldn't catch that. "Oh. I just nodded my head."

"Yeah, I got that. See-smell-feel-hear."

"Right. That makes things easier."

I stood and picked up the old lady and returned her to her bed.

Samantha popped back into my head as I was picking up Frank. "Oh, and bring some aspirin. This headache is a killer."

*

I landed in front of Los Angeles Self Storage at 3:23 in the morning. The building was a three-story-tall, climate controlled self-storage building. The street in front of it was devoid of people *and* cars, which worried me. There weren't even any cars parked out on the street. It seemed to me that people weren't ready to move back into big cities yet, despite the Richter problem having been taken care of. Maybe not enough time had passed? When I thought about it, I realized that I still didn't know how long I'd been gone. I had no idea how much time had passed, and that worried me.

I gripped the bottle of aspirin tighter in my hand and pulled the headpiece of my Tempest outfit over my face. I began walking to the front door of the building. When I reached the front door, I realized that I didn't have a key to get it. I didn't want to have to break in, but just as I was figuring out what the best and least damaging way to do so would be, the lock in the door clicked. I pulled on the door, and it opened.

"Sorry. Forgot to mention the door would be locked. Come on up," Samantha said in my head.

I tried to shake the uneasy feeling that crept into the back of my head. I had no idea what I was walking into. I knew that I shouldn't be rushing into things, but I didn't have much of a choice. I had no idea what was going on in the world, and Samantha had answers. At least she *said* she did. She'd said that even before I took out Richter, so I could only imagine what she'd learned in my absence.

Truth was, I didn't have much of a choice. Samantha had helped me take out Richter. I wouldn't have figured out how to do that on my own, and even if I had, it probably would've been too late. I owed her one, so I forced myself to enter the storage building and walk up the stairs to the third floor.

"What room is it again?" I whispered once I reached the correct floor. I looked down the row of storage unit in front of me, searching for any sign of Samantha.

A large garage door rattled down the hallway ahead of me, and the smiling face of a young lady with blonde hair pulled up into a ponytail poked out from the storage unit. "This one!" she said.

I instantly recognized the voice as Samantha's. I breathed a sigh of relief when I saw her. She didn't look crazy or anything. Although she did seem to be living in a storage unit. She smiled at me as I walked down the hallway toward the unit. Her bright blue eyes sparkled behind her thick black-framed glasses.

"You must be Samantha," I said when I reached her, sticking my hand out.

She ignored my hand. Instead, she jumped toward me and gave me a hug. I was taken aback, unsure how to respond.

"Thank you," she said. Then she pulled back and looked me up and down. "Wow. I can't believe it's really you! Thank you so much for what you did. Taking out Richter…I know it wasn't easy, but if you hadn't done something, who knows where we'd all be today."

I smiled, and a warm feeling rose within me. I couldn't help but smile. I hadn't had any time to process anything yet, and it was just now beginning to hit me what I'd done.

I really had defeated Richter. I really had saved billions of people. I was having a hard time processing it, and I had the feeling that it wouldn't get easier to do so for a while.

The weight of everything started to hit me. Dizziness washed over me, and I almost fell over. I took a step to try to stabilize myself.

"Are you okay?" Samantha asked, putting a hand on my shoulder.

I took a deep breath. "Yeah," I said. "I'm good. It's just… a lot has happened lately."

"That's definitely an understatement." She turned back into her storage unit. "Come on," she said, gesturing for me to follow. "There's a seat waiting for you in here."

CHAPTER 4

Q&A

I SHUT THE DOOR behind me with a loud *bang*. When I turned around, the smell of air freshener hit me in all of its fake-flowery glory.

"Sup? I'm Doug," I heard someone say.

I looked behind a desk and saw a kid who looked to be no older than fourteen sitting there. He had extremely curly hair, and was wearing an oversized sweatshirt that had a couple of stains on it. I was taken aback; I hadn't been expecting company. "Oh, hi. I didn't know you were in here," I said, looking to Samantha for an explanation.

"This is my little brother, Doug," Samantha said as she cleared some dirty clothes off a large recliner. Once it was clean, she stood gesturing toward it like she was a car salesperson showing off her latest import. "Here you go."

"Thanks," I said as I sat down. As soon as I hit the chair, I was overcome with drowsiness. The chair conformed to every part of my body, wrapping me in comfort. I sank into it, welcoming the warmth it provided. "Oh, wow," I said as I closed my eyes and took it in. "I didn't realize how tired I was."

"Should we leave the two of you alone?" Samantha asked from behind her own desk next to Doug's.

I smiled. "No, I'm good." I sat up in the chair and wiped the drowsiness from my eyes.

"Did you bring that aspirin?" Samantha asked.

"Oh, yeah," I said. I'd forgotten it was in my hand. The side of the chair was pushed up against the front of her desk, so I leaned over and placed the bottle down next to her keyboard.

"Thanks," she said as she popped the bottle open and poured a couple of aspirin into her hand.

I looked around the storage unit. It was actually pretty cozy in here. There were some battery-powered lamps lighting up the room, and some small fans keeping the air circulating. Doug's and Samantha's desks were in the left and right corners respectively, facing the door of the unit. There was a small gap between them so you could squeeze by and get behind their desks.

In front of the desks, besides the chair I was sitting in, were two cots with pillows and sleeping bags on top, some boxes filled with belongings, and a small battery-powered generator.

"This is some setup you got here," I said.

"Thanks," Doug said as he typed away on his laptop.

"This is just our 'office', I guess you could call it," Samantha said after she took a swig of her water. "We're 99% sure we can't be tracked, but just in case, we have this setup. We have our own apartment, too, of course."

"Oh, good. It looked like you guys might be living here," I said as I looked back at the cots and belongings.

"No, no," Samantha said with an almost embarrassed laugh. "Sometimes we have to pull all-nighters, though, so we just leave those set up."

I leaned forward in my seat. "Speaking of which, what exactly do you do? I'm guessing you have powers?"

Samantha and Doug looked at each other for an uncomfortable moment. Then Samantha turned to me. "Well, yeah, but we were actually wondering if you could maybe take your mask off? I know you want to keep your identity a secret and everything, but if we're going to just start telling you all about our powers and such, we'd kinda like to know who we're talking to."

I thought about it for a moment. That request was fair enough. If they were about to launch into a big spiel about what all they could do, they deserved to know who they were telling their biggest secrets to. I felt as if I could trust them enough to reveal my identity to them.

I slipped off my headpiece, and it hung behind me like a hood. "My name is Kane Andrews," I said, reaching my hand over Samantha's desk.

She smiled as she shook my hand. "Samantha Trask."

Doug got up from his desk and leaned over just enough to reach my hand. I reached out for him, and we shook. "Douglas Aiden Trask," he said with a goofy smile.

"Nice to meet you, Douglas."

"It's Doug."

"Of course," I said, raising my hands to concede. I sat back in my chair. "Now, what exactly do you do?"

Samantha took a quick sip of water and cleared her throat. "Well, as you've experienced, I can project myself into other people's bodies." She stopped, and made an adorable scrunched-up face. "Well, kinda. It's a lot less creepy than it sounds. Basically I can see, hear, smell, and feel anything someone else is feeling. And I can project my thoughts into their brain. Well, I can do all those things to most people. I'm still trying to get the hang of it. It's a lot easier for me to do to people I know well or see a lot. Still, it can be difficult. It took me a long time to get hold of you. I had been trying ever since I first got my powers."

"When was that?" I asked. "How long have I been gone?"

"Six months," Doug said.

"Both how long you've been gone, and how long I've had my powers. I got them the day after you caught that girl," Samantha said.

I barely paid attention to what she was saying. Doug's words haunted me.

Six months.

Six *whole* months. The fact that six months of my life were just gone made me feel incomplete. How much could I have gotten done in those six months? How much could I have changed in those six months? I felt as if I was far behind, and struggling desperately to catch up. There was so much I'd missed out on, for sure. Of all the times to spend in a comatose state on the Moon, it just *had* to be the six months that mankind was going through the biggest changes it ever had.

"I'm really good with computers," Doug blurted out. He seemed to be trying hard not to jump up and down in his seat.

I snapped back to reality. "Really? That's interesting. That's your power?"

"Yeah, that's it," Samantha said. "Well..." She looked up to the ceiling, thinking. "Okay, so it's not really a *super*power—"

"Bullshit!"

"Hey! Watch it," Samantha scowled.

"It's *definitely* a superpower," Doug said, shooting her a

sideways glance. He turned to me, and his face returned to its normal, sweet demeanor. "Just not in the traditional sense."

"Well, I'm not very good at computers, so regardless, you're better at it then I am," I said. An idea popped into my head. "Hey, can you try to find something on the internet for me?"

Doug sighed. "I mean, you don't have to be a superhero to use Google—"

"You're not a superhero," Samantha groaned.

"—*but*," Doug said, shooting her another death glare. "I'd be happy to be your personal Siri, just this once."

"Thank you, Doug," I said with a smile. He smiled back, knowing that the two of us were getting on Samantha's nerves, and thoroughly enjoying it. "Can you see if you can find some records or something that'll tell you where my parents are? Their names are Andy and Zoe Andrews."

Doug held back a laugh. "Your dad's name is Andy Andrews?"

I rolled my eyes. That was an observation I'd been hearing people make for years. "Yes."

Doug waited for me to say more, but when I didn't, he began typing away.

"So, what's happened since I've been gone?" I asked Samantha.

"Well, you picked the wrong six months to spend sleeping away," she said, echoing my earlier thoughts. "A few more Supers—which is what we're being colloquially known as—have shown up. Their powers range from flight to communicating with animals."

"Really?" I said, taken aback. "That's an interesting one. How many, exactly?"

"Seven. That we know of, at least. So all in all, there's nine of us Supers."

"Ten," Doug said under his breath.

"*Nine*. However, the number of free Supers? There's only five, including you and me. *Don't even*," she said to Doug before he could get his protest out.

"What do you mean *free*?" I asked. I had a bad feeling about what her answer was going to be.

"Every time a new Super shows up, it's not long before they disappear. One time it was a very public disappearance. A bunch of people in all black body armor pulled up in a large vehicle when this Super, who could stretch his body like elastic, was showing off his powers to a bunch of his friends. They started shooting these guns that shot out purple lighting, and knocked out the Super. They put him in the back of a van, and drove off."

"We think the government is behind the disappearance of the other Supers. So by that logic, they have four Supers in custody," Doug said.

Their words began to sink in. The government wasn't interested in killing the other Supers like they were Richter and me. Hell, I wasn't even sure they were interested in killing *me* anymore. If they were, they would've just left me on the Moon.

Shit, just thinking about being on the Moon made my stomach turn. I couldn't believe I'd spent six months up there. I'd never be able to look at the night sky the same way again.

"They would have had five, if I hadn't escaped from them," I said.

"Yeah, we figured going to get you was why the NASA shuttle program was very quickly refunded with little to no explanation. They didn't want to partner with any of the other space programs of the world, because that meant they'd have to share whatever they learned from you, or any of the Supers, presumably."

"So they didn't tell people why they were going up there?"

"Just your regular ISS spiel. Nobody believed it. though, although nobody knew you were up there, so they really weren't sure what they were going for. Just that it probably had something to do with the Supers."

"It seems like everything does these days," Doug said with a yawn.

"You tired?" Samantha asked.

"A little. It's only almost four in the morning," he said sarcastically.

Samantha sighed. "We'd better get some rest. Busy day tomorrow." She stood and began putting her laptop into her backpack. "You can stay here on one of the cots," she said.

I nodded. "Thanks, I'll do that." I settled back into the chair, enjoying the relaxation and comfort it radiated.

"Or just sleep in the chair," Doug said.

"I'll do that too," I mumbled. I was already slipping away into sleep's embrace.

"See you in a few hours," Samantha said, but before I could respond, I was already fast asleep.

CHAPTER 5
FLOOR 24

THE SOUND OF the storage unit door rolling up woke me from my sleep. I jumped up, unaware of where I was for a few moments before the memories came back to me in a hurry.

"Good morning," I said with a dry throat.

"*Afternoon,*" Samantha corrected me as she walked behind her desk. She turned some lights on and began taking her things out of her backpack.

Doug slammed the storage unit door shut, and gave me a nod as he walked by.

"How has nobody found out about you guys living in here yet?" I asked as I stood and stretched. "Somebody's gotta start getting suspicious of you guys coming and never leaving for a long time."

"It's something to do with one of my powers, I think. I'm not sure. I haven't exactly gotten the hang of it, but I can—in a way—turn myself invisible. If I can concentrate, I can get into people's minds and make them ignore me. They don't know why, but they can't look directly at me, and they don't even notice me. It comes in handy when we're sneaking in here. So to them, no one's come to this storage unit for a long time."

"Well, you failed to mention this mind control power yesterday. That and your memory erasing thing," I said as I sat back down.

"I was just trying to give you the CliffsNotes. Besides, that was the first time I'd ever successfully erased memories in a human. It's very difficult, and the fact that they were in their seventies or eighties was the only reason I was able to do it." Samantha opened her laptop and sat down. "But that's not what we're going to talk about today. We have a big opportunity on our hands that we need to take advantage of."

This piqued my interest. I got up from the chair and stood between Samantha's and Doug's desks. "Okay, what is it?"

"First, Doug?" Samantha gestured toward Doug's backpack. "Give Kane those clothes." She turned to me. "Your outfit is a little worn. We got you some fresh clothes to change into."

"Yeah, I heard wearing the same thing for six months straight isn't good for your skin," Doug said as he handed me a folded-up red t-shirt and basketball shorts.

"Thanks," I said as I grabbed them from his hands. I began to change into the clothes at super speed. I pulled off the Tempest outfit and the clothes I was wearing beneath it in one smooth motion, and put on the clothes that Doug had given me. The change happened so fast, all Doug and Samantha saw was me in my Tempest outfit one second, and the very next, I was in my fresh clean clothes.

I tossed the tattered Tempest outfit on the chair I'd slept in. Wearing the fresh, comfortable clothes felt amazing. It was like I'd shed an old, tight skin, and a fresh, loose one had grown in its place.

"I wish I could get ready in the morning that fast," Samantha said. "Okay, so, next thing. Over the past few months, Doug and I have been keeping a close eye on all the Supers. We've been tracking them, keeping logs of what they're getting into, and if they've been taken by the government, everything behind their disappearance."

I held up my hands, stopping Samantha. "I'm happy to help you guys. It's obvious that we need to figure out everything we can about all the Supers, as well as what the government's role is in all of this. But I really need to find my parents. They need to know that I'm alive and okay. I can't have them finding out I'm back through the news or something. I need to find them."

"Of course, Kane. I'm sorry. I get ahead of myself sometimes," Samantha said.

"Don't worry about it. You find anything, Doug?"

Doug nodded as he took a bite from a granola bar. "Yeah, I found something." He sat up in his chair and began messing with something on his laptop. "It looks like Mr. Andy Anderson is a practicing lawyer again." Doug turned the laptop around to face me.

I looked at the screen, and saw my dad standing in front of a podium at a press conference. I recognized the fire in his eyes. Even though it was just a picture, I could hear his voice in my head, filled with passion. He spoke with determination and ferocity.

"In the past three months, his clients have received over five million dollars in settlements. They've all been people who've lost family members or property due to Richter. Right now, lawyers are seeing a huge gold rush. Everybody's suing everybody, and your dad's doing a pretty good job making sure people are getting paid," Samantha explained.

All my attention was fixed on the picture. I smiled, feeling a weird sense of pride for my father. It's a weird feeling, being proud of your parents. I always tried really hard to make sure they were proud of me, but now my dad was out there kicking ass, doing what he loved. Even though being a lawyer—all the paperwork, red tape and such—sounded horrendously boring, if I got the chance, I would be sitting in the courtroom watching my dad do his thing in a heartbeat. There was just something about seeing my dad doing what he was passionate about that lit a fire inside of me. I wanted nothing more in that moment than to find him and give him the biggest hug that I could.

"Where can I find him?" I asked.

"He and your mother live in an apartment building in Indianapolis. The York Towers, apartment 2407," Doug said.

Seconds after he finished his sentence, I was already out of the storage unit, flying as fast as I could toward Indianapolis.

*

I stood in the lobby of the York Towers, taking in the beautiful sight. A crystal chandelier hung from the ceiling, a ceiling which had beautiful scenery painted on it a la Michelangelo and the Sistine Chapel. The only difference was that this ceiling was probably just wallpaper, not something that had taken years to paint. At the back of the lobby sat a receptionist's desk behind which were three people going about their daily work. The only other people in the lobby were sitting on the couches to my right, sipping complementary coffee, waiting for their friends to come down and meet them.

A man in a business suit talking on his phone rushed past me, fumbling with his belongings, trying to get his keycard out so he could activate the elevator he was walking toward. I fell in line behind him, keeping up with his brisk speed. The receptionists saw him coming and were getting ready to greet him when he came near. I hoped they would pay no attention to me. They would see the man was in a rush, assume I was with him, and not bother us since we were obviously busy.

We walked by the desk, and other than a quick nod, passed by without any interruptions. I smiled to myself. The man I was behind probably didn't even realize I was there. He scanned his keycard at the elevator, the doors opened, and the two of us stepped inside. He punched the button to floor 17, and I, floor 24.

Just a few more minutes and I'd be reunited with my parents. I zoned out as the floors dinged by. All I could think about was what I was going to do. What would I say? "Mom, Dad, I'm home!" Or go for a more funny and casual, "Hey, guys, what's for dinner?" Or, "You guys wouldn't believe the traffic! Took me *forever* to get to the Planet Earth exit!"

The elevator stopped at the 17th floor, and the man stepped off. The doors closed, and I was one stop away from seeing my parents. Alone in the elevator, I began pacing. The thought hit me: was this a bad idea? Were my parents safer not knowing I was back? They seemed happy, and my being with them would surely put them in danger. If anything happened to them, would I be able to live with myself? I tried to push the thoughts out of my mind, but they were already beginning to cement. They'd find out I was back eventually. It'd be all over the news when Tempest made his appearance once again. Still, was this a good idea?

The doors to the 24th floor opened, and my decision was made for me. Standing there in an immaculate business suit, talking on his cell phone, was my father.

"Hey Trev, I'm gonna have to call you back."

Dad and I stared at each other for a few moments, unable to move. We were both taking each other in. Taking the moment in. We each couldn't believe it was the other, and after having so much time to think about what we would do if we were in this situation, now that we were here, we were both frozen.

Not sensing any movement, the elevator doors began to close. We both stuck our hands in the doorway, letting out a yelp of surprise, and the doors opened.

That shook me out of my trance, and I grabbed my dad, giving him a big hug. I held him tight. Even though status quo would tell you that a seventeen-year-old was too old to be giving his dad a hug, screw that. I'd been through too much to care about the status quo.

Dad pulled away, and he began inspecting me. "Are you okay? Are you hurt? Are you in trouble?" Tears welled in his eyes.

"Dad, I'm fine." I smiled, and found tears of joy beginning to form in my own eyes. "Just glad to be home."

"You're going to have to tell me everything that happened. First, we gotta go see your mother."

He put an arm around me, and the two of us walked toward apartment 2407, father and son back together again.

Chapter 6
Comeback

I SAT AT THE kitchen table of my parents' apartment, sipping a cup of coffee. On one side of the dark wood table sat my mother, and on the other, my father. The two of them were filling me in on the past six months. Their entire bodies were animated as they spoke at a thousand miles an hour. I had to ask them to slow down a few times, but their adrenaline was rushing, and their hands were shaking, and the only way they could burn it off was by talking as fast as I could run.

Mom's reaction was about what I'd expected. Screaming, crying, screaming, crying again, and now half-crying, half-screaming as she gave me her recap.

"...and I said, 'HOW DARE YOU SAY THAT ABOUT TEMPEST! THAT'S MY *S*—', but then I remembered that, oh, duh, Zoe, nobody knows who he is!" She let out a hysterical laugh, while Dad and I forced a chuckle. Things were already getting back to normal.

"That's funny, Mom," I said. "What did you guys tell everybody about me? That could get awkward when we go back to Ebon."

"Well, we'll talk more about the going back to Ebon

situation later, but we told your friends that you were really sick. Thankfully there was a flu outbreak around town at the time, so they understood. That bought us some time, but of course not much. If we'd gone with that story any longer, they'd probably be calling the cops on us for not taking you to a hospital or something," Dad said with a laugh.

Mom chuckled too, as if that was some sort of inside joke. "So then we told them that you left to volunteer with the relief efforts in Seattle."

I had flashbacks to the last time I was in Seattle, when Richter had brought down the Space Needle on top of me.

"Yeah, they weren't too happy about that Space Needle thing, in case you were wondering," Dad said with a sly smile.

I could tell he thought the whole thing was pretty cool. I have to admit, in retrospect, that whole thing was pretty awesome. Especially since I didn't die, and Richter…he did. I hadn't really had much time to think about it, but that one thought was the straw that broke the camel's back. The floodgates opened, and it was all I could think about. I'd killed Richter. I'd killed Patrick Henry.

And strangely, I didn't feel as if I'd lose much sleep over it. It wasn't like I'd had any other choice. Besides, there was no telling how many people Richter had killed.

Two wrongs don't make a right.

I pushed the thoughts out of my head. Now wasn't the time.

"…to say, they probably aren't going to be very happy with you for disappearing on them like that. In my opinion, though, I don't think you should tell them the truth. With Supers disappearing as soon as they're showing up, it's too dangerous for them to know," Dad said.

So I was supposed to lie to them—a wrong—to keep them safe—a right.

"Yeah, I was thinking the same thing," I said, thinking back to my few moments alone in the elevator. I was glad to be back with my parents, though. Even if it was a bit selfish, even if I was putting them in danger, I'd be able to keep them safe. It'd be easy to, since they were just two people. If I had them, Macy, and Drew to look after, especially since they were spread out all across Indiana? Forget it. I couldn't be everywhere at once.

"But about Ebon," Dad began.

I didn't like where this was going. I looked away, my eyes on the TV behind him. The television was muted, and the channel was turned to a news station. I didn't need to hear to read what the ticker was telling me: *NEW SUPER EMERGES IN DALLAS, BANK ROBERY IN PROGRESS.*

"Guys," I said, standing from my seat, pointing at the TV.

Mom and Dad turned to look. Dad got up, walked over to the remote, and un-muted the television.

"…hostages. Six suspects reported in this standoff between the Supers and Dallas PD and SWAT. No word on what powers this Super possesses, but we're getting reports that this *is* the work of a Super."

"I think it's time for Tempest to make his comeback."

*

"I had a lot of time on my hands, and I knew you'd come back, so I made you a lot of these," Mom said as she opened a closet door. Inside were over a dozen immaculate Tempest outfits, ready to be put in action.

I pulled one down and slipped it off the hanger. I felt

the leather between my fingers. I could almost feel the love and passion my mother had put into making these for me. "Thanks, Mom," I said.

She gave me a hug, and I hugged her back. Her red hair got in my face, but I didn't mind. I was just happy to be back with my mom.

I pulled away and slipped the Tempest outfit on over the clothes I was already wearing. "How do I look?" I asked.

"You look like a hero," Mom said with a smile.

I smiled back, and turned to my dad. He simply gave me a thumbs up.

I walked to the front door. "Keep an eye on the TV. I think you guys are going to be in for a good show."

Dad put and arm around Mom and smiled. "I'll get the popcorn ready."

I chuckled as I walked out of the room, shutting the door behind me. With my parents at my back, I felt truly invincible. I dashed to the stairwell of the apartment building, ran down the 24 flights of stairs, and just a few seconds after saying goodbye to my parents, I was already in the air heading toward Texas once again.

Chapter 7
Teamwork

I HOVERED OVER THE First National Bank in downtown Dallas. It was sandwiched between two larger buildings, the road in front of them blocked off. Police cars were lined up in front of the buildings, behind which officers stood with their guns at the ready. Assault rifles, pistols, and shotguns were all pointed at the front of the building, which was floor-to-ceiling windows. Using my super vision, I tried to get a good look inside. I was too high up, though, and from that angle I couldn't see much. I closed my eyes and began to listen closely.

I could hear a dozen hearts beating fast. Whimpering and crying came from most of the hostages. There were six calm, regular heartbeats in the midst of the frantic ones. Those must've been from the hostage takers—the Supers.

"Kane, you in Dallas?" I heard Samantha say in my mind.

"Yeah, I'm above the building right now," I whispered, making sure Samantha would be the only one to hear me, and not any of the people a few hundred feet below me. Nobody knew I was there yet, and I wanted it to stay that way. Tempest was a hero to these people. A hero they thought was gone forever, sacrificing his life to save them. My return needed to be spectacular and unforgettable. It needed to fill people with hope. I needed to let them know that Tempest was back, and nothing could keep him down for too long.

"Okay, I have Doug pulling up what he can about the building right now. It looks as if the Super is one we've heard rumors about, but nothing concrete. The message boards Doug frequents have had some chatter about a potential Super who has the ability to split into multiple versions of himself. In the past couple of weeks he's done some small robbery jobs—a convenience store here and there. Looks like he wanted to step up his game and bit off a little more than he can chew."

"Sounds simple enough," I said. "He doesn't have any other powers that you know of?"

"Nope, but still, be careful. If you attack one of him, he could take control of another version of him and kill the hostages. You're going to have to figure out a way to take all of them out at once."

I hovered there for a moment, thinking. An idea came to mind. "Samantha, I need to figure out which one of them is the original. The Prime. If I can take him out, the others should cease to exist, right? They'll form back together?"

"Possibly. It's our best shot. How are you going to figure out which one is the right one, though?"

"I'm not, you are."

"What? How?"

"You can project yourself into the body of any *person*, right?" I asked, almost rhetorically.

"Yeah…so, theoretically, I should only be able to project myself into the body of the Prime, not his copies, since they aren't fully human," she said, having coming to the same conclusion I had.

"Exactly," I said, smiling. We were already in sync. I had a feeling we were going to work very well together.

"Okay, it's a good idea, but I can't just project into anybody. I have to know what they look like. I have to know as much as I can about them. I gotta picture them in my mind as clearly as possible before I can even begin to attempt to project myself into their mind."

I cursed under my breath.

"I heard that."

"Sorry. You can see everything I can right now, right?" I asked.

"Gimme a sec," Samantha said.

I felt a weird tingling sensation in the back of my head. Like I had a cold itch beneath the skin.

"Okay, I can see everything now. Ah, new suit. Nice."

"Focus, Samantha. If I run in the back and get a good look at them, you think it would be enough to figure out which one is the Prime?"

"I think so. His mind is spread across six different versions of himself, so it should be weak enough for me to get into just by getting a quick glimpse."

"Okay. Get ready—here we go."

I flew around to the back of the building, where I broke one of the office windows and climbed through it. I landed on the office floor, glass crunching beneath my feet.

"Holy shit, that hurt—shut up, Doug. I'm eighteen. I can curse—I'm literally getting sensations off your nerves, Kane. I can just see and hear what you do and talk to you now. That whole 'feel what you can' isn't much fun when you're punching out windows," Samantha said.

I chuckled under my breath, but didn't respond. I quietly walked across the office and slowly opened the door. Then

I looked left and right down the hallway and saw nothing. I closed my eyes and listened. All the heartbeats and breathing were coming from the left—deeper inside the bank.

I hovered a few inches off the ground and began floating down the hallway, staying as quiet as possible. When I reached the end, I peeked around the corner.

Twelve people were sitting in a circle in the break room of the bank in various states of emotion. Some of them had tears streaming down their faces, while others had stone-cold expressions, trying to stay as tough as possible.

Standing above them with their guns aimed and fingers on the triggers were five Asian men dressed all in black. They were all identical, with the same blank expression. A sixth one stood in the back, talking on a cell phone. I figured that one was the Prime, but I had to be sure.

I pulled back from the corner and put my back up against the wall.

"I got it, Kane. Give me a few moments to try to get into his head."

We don't have much time, I thought to myself, but I didn't say it, of course.

I floated there for a few moments, waiting to hear back from Samantha.

The next moment, I felt someone grab me, and then suddenly I was flying out a window in the back of the bank. The person who had me was flying up, and I was so shocked I couldn't fight back. They slammed me into the top of one of the skyscrapers in downtown Dallas.

I jumped up, ready to fight back. I looked around to see who it was that had grabbed me, but I couldn't find them.

Then, standing at the edge of the skyscraper, I saw her.

CHAPTER 8
TIMBER

THE YOUNG WOMAN stood there, her brunette hair whipping in the wind. A black mask with white stitching covered her eyes. She was wearing a white shirt beneath a black leather jacket and dark leather pants. She didn't seem to be older than twenty.

"I'll let it pass this time, since I appreciate what you did about Richter," she yelled in order to be heard above the wind. "But stay out of my territory." Then she fell backwards off the skyscraper.

I leaped off the building, searched the skies and found her flying back toward the bank. I rushed after her and reached her in a matter of seconds. I tackled her and we both landed in a back alley.

"What the hell is your problem?" she yelled at me as she stood. She pushed me back, and I slammed into the side of a building. The bricks cracked beneath me.

I pushed myself off the wall. "What the hell is *your* problem? I was about to take out those guys at the bank."

"This is my territory, *Tempest*." She said my name like it was a curse. "Stay out of it. I've got this under control."

"Who do you think I am? I'm only trying to help," I said, raising my voice.

"Oh, yeah? How do I know that?" she spat back, taking a step toward me. "Most people when they get their powers turn into mini Richters. How do I know you're not one as well? How do I know you're one of the good guys? I don't. You can't trust a Super. Now get out of here and let me handle this."

The girl flew off, but before I could give chase, Samantha popped back in.

"Okay, I—wait. Why are you in the middle of an alleyway?"

"I had a run in with that Superchick in Dallas," I said angrily.

"Oh, Holocene? Yikes. Didn't go well?"

"Samantha, just tell me which one is the Prime."

"The one in the back, on the phone. He's still on it now."

I jumped up and began flying as fast as I could toward the bank. Holocene was bursting through the front of the bank as it came into sight. I kicked into overdrive, the windows all around me shattering as the sonic boom sounded.

I passed Holocene in a blur—apparently she wasn't nearly as fast as I was, which filled me with joy. I didn't have time to maneuver through the hallways, so I slammed through the walls of the bank. I punched holes in one office after another, heading straight for the break room where Prime and his hostages were.

I slammed through the last of the office walls and saw the gathering of people before me. In the back stood Prime, still talking on his phone. I was moving so fast, none of them had even begun to react to the fact that I had just flown straight through the building. I looked behind me, and didn't see Holocene. This victory was all mine.

I reached Prime and slowed down just a little bit. With

my strength and speed, all I did was lightly poke Prime on his chest. He slammed backwards into the wall and fell to the ground, incapacitated.

I flew out the back wall of the bank and stopped myself in the alley. I ran back in through the hole I'd just made just in time to see the last of his doppelgängers get sucked into his body.

The guns they'd been holding fell to the ground with a clatter. One of the hostages snatched one of them up and pointed it at Prime.

I ran to the wannabe hero-hostage and yanked the gun from him, then threw it against the wall. I opened my mouth to say something, but was stopped by loud cracking sounds, followed by rumbling.

Holocene appeared around the corner. "Get them out of here!" she screamed as she grabbed two hostages and dashed out of the building in a blur. It wasn't until she came back seconds later for the next one that I realized what was going on and jumped into action.

I grabbed two of the former hostages, ran out the building with them, and set them down by some police officers. I ran back in, grabbed some more, and ran out. Holocene and I had the building cleared in a matter of seconds.

The building began to collapse in on itself.

Prime was still in there.

I ran in one last time as fast as I could. The building collapsed around me in slow motion. Rubble and dirt seemed to float in the air in front of me, but if I looked closely enough, I could see it slowly falling toward the ground. I ran through the holes I'd made earlier, putting together the puzzle pieces.

In my haste and need to show up Holocene, I'd caused

this. I was trying to be a hero, and instead, I'd brought down an entire building. Yeah, I'd saved the hostages, but there were a million other ways to do that that would've ended much better.

I reached Prime and stopped for a second to grab him. The collapsing ceiling was just inches from the top of my head when I started running again. I ran out the hole in the back of the building and down the alleyway to the safety of the street.

When I stopped I heard the deafening sound of the building collapsing behind me. A cloud of dust and rubble plumed through the street, and I had to cover my mouth to keep from inhaling it.

Once the worst of it had passed, I grabbed Prime and threw him over my shoulder. I ran to the police and set him down in the back of a police car.

I didn't stop for the cameras, or for thanks. I jumped into the air and flew away, trying to out-fly my embarrassment.

But no amount of flying could change the fact that my ego and I had just brought down an entire building.

Chapter 9

The Top of the Tower

I LANDED ON TOP of York Towers. It took everything I had in me to keep from punching a hole in the ground in frustration.

I felt a cool itch in the back of my head.

"Are you okay, Kane?" Samantha asked in a soft, sweet voice.

I clenched my eyes shut and sighed. "Yeah. I'd just like to be alone for a little bit."

"Okay, well, you know where to find me," she said.

I felt her presence leave my mind.

And felt another land right behind me.

I whipped around and saw Holocene storming toward me. Before I could react, she planted a solid punch straight to my face. I fell to the ground, but didn't fight back. I deserved what was coming.

"WHAT THE *HELL* WAS THAT?" she yelled. You probably could've heard her for miles.

"How did you know I was here?" was all I could say as I stumbled to my feet. I could feel the bones in my face restructuring, popping back into place. It was a strange sensation, right on the edge of being painful. Like popping your knuckles. It was a feeling that I kinda missed.

"I followed you, dumbass. I don't want to ever see you within a hundred miles of Dallas again," she fumed. Her cheeks were turning red with anger.

"I was only trying to help, alright? I've been out of the game for a while. I'm a little rusty," I snapped back.

"Yeah? Well, leave the helping to the heroes, alright? Go back to whatever beach you've been kicking back on for the past six months, and stay out of my way."

Holocene turned around to fly off.

"I've been in a coma for six months," I said. Holocene stopped. "Killing Richter took a lot out of me, and without oxygen, it took longer for my body to repair itself. It wasn't even fully repaired until I came back to Earth on a NASA shuttle."

Holocene turned. "You mean you've been in space for the past six months?"

I nodded. "Yeah, so I'm sorry if I don't know exactly how things work. To me, it's only been a few days since I took out Richter. It's a whole new world, and I'm still trying to figure it out."

Holocene sighed. "Well, first thing you need to learn is that you're not the only Super anymore. There's a few of us, and more all the time. So going around like you're head honcho? That's not going to work. There is no hierarchy. You're either a hero or you're not. Most Supers fall into the latter."

"Don't worry, I'm a hero."

"Are you?"

I was taken aback by Holocene's accusation. "Of course

I am. I saved everyone from Richter. I saved those hostages today—even if it wasn't the way I would've liked."

Holocene looked me up and down and shrugged. "You taking out Richter? The way I look at it, that was just you doing what needed to be done. You were forced to be a hero. Had you not been, he would've kept on with his rampage until there wasn't anyone left on Earth. You didn't really have much of a choice. So if you think you've proven anything, you haven't. Not to me. To me, whether or not you're a hero or a villain is still up in the air." She walked to the edge of the building and was about to jump off. "There's no Richter anymore. There's no one to decide who you are for you. Hero or not, it's up to you now, Tempest."

Chapter 10
Ghosts

DIRECTOR LOREN SAT behind the desk in her bare office. No paintings or pictures adorned her walls and desk. There was nothing in her office that would've led anyone to believe it was the office of one of the most important people in the United States government. She was the head of the recently sanctioned, top secret government agency STF—the Super Task Force. It was the job of Director Loren and her agency to track down all Supers and bring them in to be experimented on. Figure out what made them tick. What made them *super.* It was a job she'd been very good at. She'd gotten the position thanks to how well she'd handled the Richter/Tempest situation.

She smiled as the memory came back to her. How she'd convinced Tempest to fight for them, how she'd almost taken the two of them out at once.

Almost. That was the word that haunted her. Tempest had still carried out his own mission successfully. Hers? Not quite. Well, she wouldn't make the same mistake twice. Soon, if she had her way, all the Supers would be gone. There were a few people up in Washington who wanted to try to train a few of them for their own special uses, but Loren would have none of it. She'd seen what the Supers could do, as had most of the world. No matter what it took, the Supers would be eradicated. The world was a safer place without them. No person deserved so much power. She wouldn't have a repeat of the Richter Crisis.

She'd made good progress toward her goal, though. They'd been able to learn a lot from the few Supers they'd captured. They'd even been able to develop a weapon that was—for lack of a better term—a nuclear Taser. She smirked at the thought of the name. There was even some truth to it. The tiny radioactive particles that mixed with the electricity incapacitated a Super, frying his or her brain, paralyzing them and preventing them from using their powers. It wasn't permanent, however. It couldn't be. Not yet. Her people had yet to find out everything they needed to know about the Supers. They had to learn everything they could about them to make sure there would never be another one ever again. Once she was sure there was nothing else to learn, *then* she would give the order: the execution of all Supers.

Her head tingled at the thought. She would be infamous then. The woman who'd saved the world from the Supers. A *true* hero.

She couldn't wait for that day.

That's the day you're going to have to look for a new job, she thought with a slight chuckle. She'd be happy to join the unemployment line.

A knock at the door broke her from her train of thought. "Come in," she said.

Agent York stepped into the room. "Are you busy, ma'am?"

"I am not. What have you got for me, York?"

Agent York stepped into the room and sat down in the chair across from her. "We've gone through all the details about Tempest that were transmitted to us before the shuttle went down. Really, it was just pictures of his face, fingerprints, et cetera. All the blood samples and everything else they gathered about him were destroyed in the crash."

Director Loren sat up in her chair, preparing herself for what Agent York had to tell her next. She tried to hold back a smile, but she knew what was coming. She was about to get him. She was about to learn who Tempest was. "You ran the pictures through facial recognition, yes? The fingerprints?"

Agent York nodded, but hesitated to speak. "Y-yes, ma'am. We did."

Loren didn't like the hesitation. This should be great news—fantastic news. News that Agent York should be bursting at the seams to tell her. "What is it? Who is Tempest?"

Agent York let out a deep breath. "We ran all the identifying information we have on him through the database. We ran it a dozen times. I *personally* ran it. Nothing. This guy's a ghost. He's not in any databases. Not in ours, or any other government's."

Director Loren sat back in her chair and closed her eyes. Anger welled up within her. All that work retrieving Tempest, and all they'd managed to do was set him free into the world once again. The things they were going to learn from him—the *answers* they would get… He was the most powerful of all the Supers, and he'd slipped through her fingers.

She should've captured him when she had the chance, back during the Richter crisis. She knew that she'd had no way of doing so then, but still, she kicked herself for not thinking of something.

"Agent York," Loren said as she opened her eyes and looked at York's worried face. "Get out of my office."

"Yes, ma'am. Sorry, ma'am," York said as he stood from his chair and backed out of the room.

He shut the door behind him and left Loren alone in her small, bare office.

Director Loren wished she had some pictures on her desk, or paintings on the wall. Not because looking at them would calm her down, but because she wanted nothing more than to grab something and throw it against the wall. She wanted to break something. To destroy something.

Her intercom buzzed. "Director Loren?"

Loren picked up the phone. "Yes, Sierra?"

"We have that new Super arriving from Dallas. He's being unloaded and brought to cell 903," Sierra said, her voice calm and professional.

"No, take him to the Chamber, and tell Dr. Finn not to begin the therapy until I get there. I want to do it personally," Loren said.

"Yes, ma'am. I'll be sure they're waiting for you."

"Thank you, Sierra," Loren said.

She hung up the phone as a bit of sadistic joy washed over her. She'd get her chance to break something, that was for sure. She'd get to take out her anger and frustration about her failures with Tempest on some*thing*. This new Super, coming from Dallas. A Duplicator, if she remembered correctly.

The more the merrier, she thought as she grabbed her coat from the back of her chair. She slipped it on and exited her office.

Part II:
The Rise of a Hero

Chapter 11

Riptide

September 20th, 2078

LEOPOLD RENNER TRIED to think back to the events that had led to his bleeding out on the floor of Tempest Memorial Museum. It was all he could do to try to stay awake. The darkness was always there, pulling him in. But he had to fight it. He didn't want to die. He couldn't die.

And it seemed like someone was trying to save him.

Leopold's eyes grew heavy. He'd barely had any sleep last night. Just a bit here and there. Nothing substantial, though, and he felt the drowsiness hitting him in waves. It felt like he was being washed out to sea by the rip currents. He was fighting to stay afloat, even though in the back of his mind he knew the best thing to do would be to relax. To let it take him.

The young woman he'd heard called Cassidy fell to the ground next to him. He looked into her eyes and saw fear. She reached up, clicked something behind her ear, and screamed, "GAMMA BASE INFILTRATED BY TEMPEST. HE'S TAKING EPSILON. SI—"

A gunshot rang out, causing Leopold to jump. The smell

of gunpowder brought back memories of his own injuries, and the pain in his torso roared to life.

He looked into Cassidy's dead eyes as blood dripped onto her face.

Her body disappeared.

Leo wanted to yell out in shock, but instead, he yelled in pain.

Kane Andrews picked him up, sending flashes of pain searing through his body. Kane threw Leo over his shoulder and began to run out the front door of the museum as fast as he could.

"Door, open!" Kane shouted.

Leo heard the hiss of a car door opening, and his world tumbled around as Kane put him down in the backseat of a car.

The face of a beautiful woman with brunette hair filled his vision. He recognized her from somewhere, but couldn't quite put his finger on it.

"Go, Kane!" she shouted as Kane got into the driver's seat.

The car jerked forward as they took off. Leo heard bullets ding off the side of the car as they sped to God knew where.

The woman ripped open Leopold's shirt, exposing his wounds. "He's not looking good, Kane. He's lost a lot of blood."

"We can't lose him, Selene!"

"I'm trying!"

"Samantha! We're heading for the extraction! We've got him, but he's been shot!" Kane shouted.

"Just keep him alive until you're out of there!" the girl Leopold assumed was Samantha replied.

His vision flickered. *Sorry, guys,* he thought. *Don't know if I can do that.*

He closed his eyes, and let the riptide take him out to sea.

Chapter 12
The Statue

January 31st, 2016

IT'D BEEN A week since I destroyed the First National Bank in downtown Dallas. A week since my discussion with Holocene. A week of being scared out of my mind. I couldn't help but think about what she'd told me. Hero, or villain? I *wanted* to be a hero, but so far, I'd only caused destruction. Not just the bank, but back in my battles with Richter. Not to mention the fact that I'd killed Richter. Could I call myself a hero if I killed my enemies?

I looked up at the bronze statue of myself. At my feet, fountains shot into a pool. The statue had been put up on the UCLA campus shortly after my disappearance, once everyone knew Richter was gone for good. Apparently, there were several of them around the country. This one was the only one I'd seen, though. The only one I'd wanted to see.

I wasn't sure if I deserved it. Holocene had said I was a hero because I had to be one. I was forced to. She didn't know that I hadn't even killed Richter myself. I wouldn't have known what to do if it weren't for Samantha. Had Holocene known that, she *really* wouldn't be a fan of Tempest.

"Hey, there. Looks like they went a little generous on the jaw line, don't you think?" I heard a familiar voice say. This time, it was behind me, not in my head.

I turned around and saw Samantha bundled up in a coat. It was dark out, and Los Angeles could get surprisingly chilly at night in the winter. I smiled and patted the seat on the bench next to me. She came and sat down.

"Sorry I haven't checked in lately," I said.

"Don't worry about it. I can only imagine what you're going through," Samantha said as she rubbed her hands together.

"How'd you know I was here?"

Samantha looked at me with an expression that said, *'How do you think?'*

"Right." I tapped my temple. "You shouldn't get into people's heads without permission, you know," I said, half-joking, half-serious.

"You shouldn't go a week without checking in with your friends, you know," she fired back.

I conceded. "Fair enough."

"Speaking of which, have you been back to Ebon yet? I'm sure your friends would like to see you."

I got the sense she was ignoring the elephant in the room, like why I'd been gone for a week, or why I was staring at a statue of myself.

I shook my head. "I'm going back to school tomorrow, so I'll see them then."

"That should be fun, although probably a bit awkward."

"Yeah," I said. I wasn't sure what else to say. I was expecting the worst at school the next day, that's for sure. Dad had

had all the homework sent to him while I was gone, and had done the work for me. I'd spent a lot of the past week going over everything so I would be as caught up as possible, but it had been difficult, since my mind was either on what Holocene had said, or on school itself, not the work.

"You know, I think we can do good together," Samantha said. "And, no, I didn't mean *well.* I mean we can actually do some good. We can be heroes."

I sighed and turned back to the statue. It showed me giving an uppercut to the air. Everybody knew who I was really giving the uppercut to: Richter. That was the first punch I ever dealt to him: that uppercut in the parking lot of Ebon High School. I remembered every second of it, the way it had felt to finally hurt someone who everyone said couldn't be hurt. To do the impossible.

I liked that feeling. The feeling of giving people hope.

"I think we can, too," I said.

"Yeah?" Samantha said. "Well, good. Besides, no one knows you're back yet, anyway. No one knows it was Tempest who brought down that building."

That brought the idea that I'd been mulling over in my head back to the forefront. It was something I hated to do, but if I was going to prove to Holocene, the world, and to myself that I was a hero, it needed to be done. "Not yet, at least. I'm going to take credit for it, though. I'm going to apologize, and do whatever I can to help clean up and rebuild." It was just a small building. Small potatoes compared to what Richter had done. Still, it was the right thing to do.

"Good, I'm glad. I was hoping you'd say that," Samantha said. She stood up. "Come on, let's get out of here. I'm starving. I'll call Doug and the three of us can go get something to eat."

I stood up and nodded. "Sounds good to me. Will your parents let Doug come out, though? It's getting kind of late."

Samantha's expression turned sad. "I'm his legal guardian. My parents… They, um… They died. So…"

"Oh my gosh, I'm so sorry, Samantha," I said. Heat rushed to my cheeks from embarrassment.

"No, no, it's okay. I should've said something sooner." Samantha tried to laugh it off, but I could tell she was uncomfortable. "Actually, you know what, it is kinda late. Doug has school tomorrow too. I should get going."

"Samantha, I'm sorry I—"

"Don't worry about it, Kane," she said. She put a hand on my arm. "Have a good day back at school. If you get bored during class, or need the answers to something, send me a text. I'll see what I can do," she said with a sad smile and a wink.

"Okay, yeah, I'll do that," I said.

Samantha turned around and walked away. I saw her wipe something from her eyes, and I knew it was tears. I felt a pit in my stomach. I felt miserable, and the thought of having to go to school tomorrow made it worse.

Chapter 13
The First Day

I WAS STANDING A few hundred feet from the entrance to Ebon High School. It'd been ten months since the last time I'd been there for school. I was there a lot during the summer volunteering at the relief center in the gym—the one Richter and I later literally brought the roof down on. I hadn't thought about that for a long time. I could see that repairs had been halted, so it just sat there, the hole in the roof like a gaping wound.

Most of the people who ran construction companies had moved to bigger cities, where they were in very high demand. Lawyers and people who owned construction companies were the two groups of people who were benefiting handsomely from the Richter crisis.

People walked past me, ignoring me, off in their own worlds. They were on their phones, talking with their friends, or listening to their music. I took a deep breath, soaking in my surroundings. The chilly February air bit at the parts of my body not covered by a jacket or hat. The smell of car exhaust filled my nose as people sat in the warmth of their running cars until the absolute last second. After that, they'd be kept warm by their frantic running as they tried to get to class in time, as if it were a race or a game.

I wished making it to class in time was the worst of my troubles. I really didn't even want to come back to school, but Mom and Dad had insisted. They'd said I needed to keep up appearances, and the distraction would be good for me. I needed to be as much as a normal teenage boy as possible. So, yeah, they promptly shut down my suggestion of dropping out and getting my GED.

Deep down, I was happy they'd done that. After tossing and turning all night, I'd finally decided that I would own the situation and force myself to be excited about the distraction. I couldn't find it in me to be excited about seeing Macy and Drew again, though. I dreaded it with every fiber of my being. I had no idea how they'd react, so I expected the worst. I expected them to be mad at me, to hate me. I wasn't sure if I could blame them, either. I'd just up and disappeared for six months without so much as a goodbye. It hadn't been my choice, of course, but nonetheless it was what had happened.

I thought back to the last time I'd seen Macy. I'd dropped her off after Michael's funeral, the day she and Drew got into their big fight. She'd kissed me on the cheek, as a kiss on the lips on such an occasion seemed inappropriate. Still, she'd made me forget about my sadness, even just for a second.

And then I left. For six months.

I dreaded seeing her face again. I couldn't face her after what I'd done—even though I'd saved her life. More than once!

I sighed in frustration and watched as my breath dissipated in the cold air. I forced myself to take one step forward. And then another.

Before I knew it, I was entering the hallways of Ebon High School, beginning my senior year.

Go Eagles.

*

First and second period went by without turmoil. Some people were happy to see me, asked where I'd been, what I'd been up to, if I had any stories, etc. People I didn't really know or care about, or they me. They were probably just gathering seeds of rumors that they'd spread like wildfire. I expected by the end of the school day to hear, "Kane went to Seattle, has a Super baby mama, and contracted some sort of Super STD so now he *literally* shits fire," or something to that effect.

I sat at my desk in third period, waiting for class to start, trying to think of what I would call this super-STD—because what else are you supposed to do while waiting for class to begin? I came up with a few, but my best by far was *firerrhea.*

"Kane?" I heard someone say, breaking me from my train of thought.

I looked up, and standing there—*with facial hair*—was Drew. "You have facial hair!" I exclaimed. Not what I had imagined would be the first thing I'd say when I saw Drew again.

"You still don't!" he smirked.

Yeah, six months on the moon and not even a five o'clock shadow.

I stood up from my desk and walked over to Drew. I wasn't sure if we were about to shake hands, hug it out, or if he was going to deck me. Thankfully, he went with the option behind door number two.

He gave me a big bro-hug, patting me on the back. I patted him back, maybe just a little too hard.

"Geez, you been working out?" he asked as he pulled away, wincing as he rolled his shoulders.

"Just what happens when you're cleaning up someone else's mess," I said with a laugh. *Yes*. Already mentioning my stint in Seattle, hopefully making the whole thing more believable.

I sat back down at my desk, and Drew sat in the one next to me. "Not even a postcard?" he said.

"Sorry, bro. I was very busy, to say the least."

"Oh, I'm sure. I went out and volunteered in New York, actually," he said.

"Really? That's awesome! How long were you out there?" I asked. I got a little lightheaded. If Drew had volunteered in the relief efforts, he'd know how everything was run. He'd be able to see right through my bullshit. I made a mental note that I'd have to get a phone call every time he wanted to trade war stories.

"I got back after Christmas. What made you stay in Seattle for so long?" he asked, looking at me curiously.

I looked down at the open notebook in front of me, trying to think of an answer. "Oh, you know, they really did a number up there. That whole Space Needle thing, especially."

"Huh," Drew said. He began getting his things from his pack. "Well, good to have you back. Really missed you, dude."

I smirked and nodded. "Yeah, it feels really good to be back."

Our teacher, Mr. Haver, walked into the classroom and began writing something on the board. I got my pen out, ready to take notes.

One down, one to go.

*

It was lunchtime, and Drew and I decided we'd eat in the cafeteria instead of going out to get lunch. We found an empty table near the back of the cafeteria and sat down across from each other.

"So, do you know where Macy's at? I feel like I should hurry up and let her know I'm here. If I go the whole day without saying hi, she might kill me," I said with a nervous laugh.

I didn't like the look Drew gave me. "We don't really hang out anymore, so I'm not sure. She's probably sitting somewhere with her boyfriend…sorry."

My heart dropped, and my mind raced. I hadn't expected her to wait for me after being gone for six months, but I was hoping I could find my way back into her life one way or the other. But she had a boyfriend now, and that meant that she was off limits—both as a friend or anything more. She was probably way over me, and I knew that if I tried being friends with her, her boyfriend probably wouldn't like that.

If she knew who I was, though, why I'd left, she'd understand. If I told her I'd been in a coma, she definitely wouldn't. But that wouldn't be the right thing to do. Stealing someone's girlfriend wasn't the hero thing to do.

I really hated trying to be a hero at that moment. It was like I was on a diet or something. I knew it was good for me, I knew it was a thing I could do, and I knew that it was what I needed to do. Still, I felt the urge to indulge myself, and I found that denying that was a very hard thing to do.

"Who's her boyfriend?" I asked as nonchalantly as I could. I took a bite of my chocolate pudding.

"Yeah, well, that's the kicker," Drew said. He looked down

at his plate, thinking for a moment. Then he looked up at me, wincing. "Brian Turner."

I almost spit out my pudding. I swallowed hard. "*Brian Turner*? Holy. Shit. I...I mean...holy *shit*!"

"Keep your voice down!" Drew said, trying to calm me down.

A million thoughts assaulted my brain at once. The biggest of which was disbelief. "He's the biggest asshole of all time! He bullied me for *years*!"

Drew shrugged and took a bite from his mashed potatoes as if it was all old news. "That alley incident last year knocked a few screws loose or something. He's like a giant teddy bear now. Everybody loves him. He loves everybody. He's like the Buddha of Ebon High."

Even though my mind was in a frenzy, Drew's humor penetrated my thoughts, and I could help but laugh. "I'm sure he loves that nickname."

"That's the thing!" Drew said incredulously. "He doesn't care! You could go up to him and say, 'Hey, Brian, just wanted to let you know that your mom's the fattest person ever, and your sister's a whore—I'd know,' and he wouldn't care."

I winced at Drew's example.

"Yeah, well, we can't all bat a thousand," he said with a sigh.

I laughed, as did Drew. I felt my guard falling down, like I was becoming Kane Andrews again. Sitting in the cafeteria with Drew, laughing about Brian, felt normal. Well, almost. There was an empty seat next to Drew where Michael would have sat, and in the back of my mind, I wished he was there. I would've loved to hear what he had to say about Drew's lackluster insults.

"There's a party tonight at Zach's place, if you wanna come," Drew said, changing the subject.

"A party on a Monday night?" I asked, giving him a look.

"His parents are out of town but just for tonight, so pretty much yeah. Nothing too crazy, though, just hanging out and stuff. Chilling."

"Sure, I guess," I said. It wouldn't hurt anything.

"Cool. Where're you living? Want me to pick you up?"

"Huh? What?" I asked, but then I remembered. He must've heard about Mom and Dad selling the farm. "Oh, we live in an apartment downtown," I said. "I remember how to get there, though."

"That's pretty cool about your dad. He's a pretty good lawyer, I hear. I'm glad you guys decided to move back to Ebon."

"Yeah, there's no place like home."

CHAPTER 14
S&T, LLC

I WALKED INTO APARTMENT 2407 at the York Towers in downtown Indianapolis—home sweet home.

"I'm home, Mom," I called.

Mom peeked out of the kitchen, which sat to the right of the front door. "How was school?"

I set my backpack down on the couch and walked into the kitchen, where I got a glass of water. "Fine. Drew was cool, didn't ask too many questions."

"And Macy?"

I didn't want to answer that question. "She's good, I guess."

"You guess?" Mom stopped making her protein shake. "You mean you didn't talk to her?"

I shrugged as I placed my glass in the sink. "She's dating Brian Turner, and we didn't have any classes together, so not really. I flew home right after class was over."

"Oh, honey," Mom said. She looked at me with pity in her eyes. "I'm so sorry."

"It's okay, Mom. Really."

I heard a door close down the hall. I hadn't been aware anyone else was home. I looked out the kitchen doorway and saw Dad come walking down the hallway and into the living area.

"You're home from work already?" I asked.

"I took off early. Wanted to be here when you got home," he said. He leaned up against the back of the couch, crossing his arms.

I walked out and climbed up to sit on the bar that extended from the kitchen to the living area. I swung my feet back and forth beneath me.

"How was school?" he asked.

"Fine, I guess. Nothing special."

"Macy's dating Brian Turner," Mom said.

"Zoe," Dad said, giving her a look that simply said, *'Really?'* "You okay with that?"

"Yeah, it's whatever, Dad," I said. I really didn't want to talk about it. "I didn't even get the chance to talk to her, anyway."

"Not even a hello?"

"Nope. I might see her tonight, though. I'm going to a party."

"On a Monday night?" Dad asked, surprised.

"Well, it's not really a party. Just hanging out and stuff."

"Well, make sure you're not out too late. You don't have homework, do you?"

"Yeah, but I'll get it done before I leave."

Dad nodded, satisfied with my answer. "Well, I'm gonna head up to the office and try to get some work done." He grabbed his briefcase from the bar next to me.

"Drop me off at the gym on your way, will ya?" Mom asked as she walked out of the kitchen, protein shake in hand.

"Of course, sweetie," Dad answered.

The two of them walked to the front door. Before they left, Dad turned to me. “Make sure that homework’s done before you leave.”

“I will, Dad,” I said as I got down from the bar.

“Hey, keep your head up, Kane. Everything’ll be fine.”

I nodded in acknowledgement. “Thanks, Dad.”

He shut the door behind him, and I started working on my homework, getting ready for the party.

*

Usually, the flight from Indianapolis to Ebon didn’t take me very long at all. But this time, I was taking my time. Almost every time I flew, it was as fast as I could. Slowing down to *soar* was an incredible feeling. Something I wished I could do more often. I watched as the city lights passed beneath me, like veins leading toward the beating heart of Indianapolis. Cars passed by below, their drivers unaware of the superhuman Tempest flying above them.

I was thankful for the cold winter air, as that meant I had an excuse to wear long-sleeved shirts and jackets. That meant I could wear my Tempest outfit under my clothes, which I found surprisingly comfortable. It kept me *very* warm.

“Hey, there. Just checking in,” I heard Samantha say in my mind.

“Howdy, pardner,” I said with a chuckle. The relaxation of flying had lifted my spirits a considerable amount.

“Anything to report on the school front?”

“Not what I had in mind for senior year, but it wasn’t a complete disaster.”

“That’s good to hear. I was hoping to hear from you today,

but I realized I never gave you my number. It was a slow day here at Tempest & Samantha, LLC, HQ."

"That's a lot of acronyms."

"Yeah, it's a work in progress."

I gave Samantha my number and felt my phone vibrate in my pocket as she sent me a text, giving me her number.

"If you find yourself in a sticky situation, just send me something and I'll be there in a flash."

"That's good to know," I said with a smile. It really was nice to think about. If I ever needed someone to talk to, I had the voice in my head—and I wasn't crazy, which made it that much better.

"Doug and I had a bit of a breakthrough today while we were going over our files on the Supers so far. It's kinda embarrassing that we didn't see it before. When can you come by Samantha & Tempest, LLC, HQ?"

"What happened to Tempest & Samantha?"

"Yeah, I decided that since I pay the rent, my name goes first."

"Fair enough. I'm on my way to hang out with my friends. I'll be by later tonight. Sound good?" I said. Speaking of which, I saw the lights of Ebon twinkling in the distance.

"Sounds good. I'll be here waiting."

"Okay, well, I'm almost in Ebon. I'll talk to you later."

"Later," Samantha said. With that, she left my mind.

I pulled my phone out of my pocket and looked at the time. I decided to pick up the pace a little bit.

A few minutes later, I landed outside Zach's house and walked inside.

Chapter 15
Weak Secrets

I WALKED INTO ZACH'S foyer, noting the bowl filled with people's car keys. My stomach turned at the thought of drinking and flying. I would definitely be throwing up all over Indiana.

Don't drink and fly, kids.

"Hey, man, good to see you," Drew said when he saw me walk in.

I gave him a fist bump. "Alright, tell me straight: is Macy here?"

"Macy and her beau," Drew said with an elbow prod.

The lack of amusement on my face showed Drew that I wasn't quite ready to be cracking jokes about the whole situation.

"Yeah, she's here," Drew said.

I sighed. "I should probably get this over with, right?"

"I would. Treat it like a Band-Aid. Just rip it off, fast and hard."

"Good talk," I said as I walked past Drew and into Zach's living room.

I was greeted by a chorus of *heys*, *long time no sees*, and

Where the hell have you been? I did my best to answer the questions as succinctly as possible, but my attention was elsewhere. Across the living room, alongside the fireplace, stood Macy. Her ginger hair was pulled up into a ponytail, and she was sipping from a cup in her hand. She looked at me out of the corner of her eye, making no effort to speak to me. She was waiting for me to make the first move.

Brian Turner, however, saw me, and let out a big smile. "Kane Andrews!" he shouted. He walked over to me and gave me a fist bump. "It's good to see you, bro!"

I thought back to what had happened the last time Brian and I talked at a party. He'd thanked me for saving his life by calling an ambulance when he was lying broken in an alley. He had no memory that *I* was the one who had put him there in the first place. I was the one who'd changed Brian from being a big bully to the apparent teddy bear he was today. The Buddha of Ebon High. I could almost feel the salt being poured onto my wounds. It was bad enough that Macy was dating my enemy, but I was the one who had made him the person he was today—the person Macy had apparently fallen in love with.

"Good to see you too," I lied.

I looked over his shoulder at Macy. She looked down and began to inspect her drink when she saw me looking at her.

"Hey, Macy," I said.

She looked up at me. "Hi." Then she turned back to her drink.

Ouch.

I'd had enough. I walked past Brian and right over to Macy. "Can we talk?"

"Fine."

Without looking back, the two of us walked through the kitchen and out the back door.

I shut the door behind me, and when I turned around, Macy slapped me hard across the face.

"I deserved that," I said.

"You deserve worse, Andrews," she spat.

I fought the urge to wince. She wouldn't even use my first name. "Look, I'm sorry, alright? I was going through a rough time, with Michael and everything. I just needed some space."

Macy slapped me again, this time harder. Tears welled in her eyes. "How *dare* you use Michael as an excuse like that? You could've called. You could've texted. Hell, get out a pen and paper and write a goddamn letter, I don't care. You have no excuse, Andrews. No excuse. None that I'll accept, anyway. You're just an asshole, and I'm through talking to you. Just leave me alone." Macy pushed me aside and started to open the door.

I grabbed the doorknob and shut it. "Macy, please. Just listen to me, alright? I can explain." My brain was telling me to shut up, but my heart ignored it. I was prepared to tell Macy everything. To show her the Tempest suit I had on under my clothes and explain everything.

"Get out of my way, Andrews," she said, pushing me back. She opened the door, slipped through, and slammed it in my face before I could react.

Then she screamed.

CHAPTER 16

PARTY CRASHERS 2.0

I SWUNG OPEN THE door and saw the living room engulfed in flames. I stood there for a few moments, stunned. People were clambering over furniture and each other, trying to get out of the house.

"Brian!" Macy yelled, and began running toward the living room.

That was when I saw it. The fire had come from a person engulfed in flames—Brian Turner.

"Oh god, help me! What's happening?" he screamed. He reached out to someone, and a torrent of flames shot from his hand, igniting the couch. Luckily the person he'd been reaching for was fast enough to run out of the way.

I wrapped my arms around Macy and lifted her up. She punched and kicked, trying to get free, but it made no difference to me.

"Put me down, Kane! I have to help!" she yelled.

I didn't listen. I took her out the back door and set her down. She tried to get past me, but there was no way I was letting her back in.

"Go get help," I said. She looked at the door behind me,

trying to see Brian through the window. "Macy! Go get help!" I yelled.

She nodded, tears streaming from her eyes. "What are you going to do?"

"I'm going to try to find a hose or something," I lied.

Macy nodded again and got out her phone as she ran to the front of the house. Once she was out of sight, I ripped off my outer clothes and revealed the Tempest outfit I was wearing underneath. I pulled the hood up, my eyes began to glow, and I ran back into the house.

The house was an inferno. Brian was running around wildly, trying to put out the flames that covered his body. From the way they shot from his body, it was clear that he wasn't just on fire, he was the source of the flames.

Brian Turner was a Super.

"Hey, kid!" I shouted, being sure to disguise my voice and making sure I didn't use Brian's name.

When he turned to look at me, his face looked like it was made of lava. Flames licked from the top of his head like they were now his hair. "Help me!" he shouted.

I reached into my pocket, and as fast as I could, sent Samantha a one-letter text. I looked around for a fire extinguisher while I waited for her to respond. I dashed to the stove and looked in the cabinet beneath it. There sat a small fire extinguisher, not nearly big enough to take on the inferno Brian was creating. It was worth a shot, though.

I grabbed it and began spraying it onto him. The foam didn't even reach him. It all evaporated almost as soon as it left the canister.

"It's not working!" Brian cried.

"What's up?" Samantha said in my head.

"I need you to see!" I shouted.

More flames erupted from Brian, burning a hole in the ceiling. I could hear people screaming outside in fear.

I felt the tingling.

"Holy shit, that's not good," Samantha said when she saw what I could.

"I'm going to try to grab him," I told her. "Take him to water."

I ran toward Brian, everything around me turning to slow motion. I watched as another plume of flame unfurled from his hand, reaching for the wall, ready to punch a hole through it with its force and heat.

I reached out for Brian. I could almost make out the fear and confusion radiating from his glowing orange eyes. I felt searing heat as I got closer and closer, the skin on my hands melting and immediately beginning to repair itself again. My hands touched Brian, and I screamed out in pain. The heat was so intense, I felt my suit begin to melt. It was almost as bad as the nukes I'd experienced when I was battling Richter.

I slammed through the wall of Zach's house, leaving Brian behind. I fell to the ground, skidding across Zach's yard, leaving a trench in my wake. I screamed in pain, and heard answering screams from the people gathering at the front of the house.

I looked down. My hands were gone. They had been completely melted away by Brian. I panicked, screaming loudly, "Holy shit!"

The bones started to regrow. Fifteen more seconds, and the flesh began to grow back. My hands tingled as the skin grew over the flesh. I had my hands back, but Brian was still on fire. If he didn't get it under control soon, I was afraid of what might happen to those who didn't have the same healing powers I did.

"Open to suggestions," I said, speaking to Samantha.

"I'm trying, I'm trying!"

Another explosion erupted from the house. I could hear sirens coming in the distance. I wasn't sure how much longer the house would last.

"Okay, Doug says to run circles around him as fast as you can. It'll create a vacuum, sucking out all the oxygen. Without oxygen, there's no fire."

As Samantha finished her sentence, I was already running back into the house through the hole I'd created. I got as close as I could bear to Brian, and began running as fast as I could.

I ran circles faster and faster. A sonic boom shook the house, breaking everything that was fragile nearby. The house seemed to hold up, though, so I didn't have to worry about the place crashing down on us.

Faster and faster I ran, my eyes focused straight ahead of me. The fire seemed to be receding back toward Brian, and his glow was diminishing. I thought it was working, but I was moving so fast, I couldn't tell. To me, everything was slowed down.

I began to slow my speed, and things around me started to speed up. The flames sucked back inside Brian, and he stopped glowing. He fell to the ground, and I stopped running.

Most of the fire in the house had dissipated—only a few small ones remained here and there.

Brian's body was black and covered in soot. Ash rained down on us, and the house groaned. I had to get him out of there and fast.

I picked him up and ran outside just as the house began to

collapse on itself. I brought him out to the road where the fire trucks and ambulances were arriving.

I set him down on the curb, and people from the party rushed over.

"Stop! Give him some space," I shouted. Everyone froze, staring at me. Seconds later, phones were out, flashes blinding my glowing eyes.

An unmarked van pulled up, peeling to a stop just a few feet away. The doors opened, and soldiers in black came pilling out of the back of the van.

"Everybody get down!" they shouted, waving their guns around. The partiers complied.

"Who are you?" I asked, struggling to see around the flashing lights from the different emergency response vehicles.

"We said get down!" one of them shouted.

"Look, I don't know who you think you a—"

One of them fired at me, purple electricity shooting from his gun. I did a back flip off the ground, the electricity traveling just beneath me. I landed in a crouched position, and the bolt of electricity hit the house behind me, sending a section of it to the ground.

The whole team opened fire. I flew into the air, dodging each bolt of electricity with ease. But there were too many of them. I couldn't keep my eye on every one.

"Kane, get out of there! Trust me, do it!" Samantha shouted at me.

I didn't know what to do. I couldn't leave my friends with these crazy people with the guns, but Samantha didn't seem to think I could take them down.

I couldn't give up. I began flying toward the company of soldiers, ready to take them down with ease.

Until one of the bolts hit me square in the chest.

I lost all control of my body.

I went rigid, and felt myself begin to fall toward the ground. I still had all of my forward momentum, however, and went flying straight through the second floor of the house across the street.

I slammed through the house, every hit sending shockwaves of pain through my body. Then I exited out the other side and slammed into the ground.

I lay in the backyard, broken. I couldn't move voluntarily. My body spasmed as the electricity from the bolt continued to course through me. I felt it traveling through my head, down my arms, across my chest—in every fiber of my being.

It dissipated, and I lay there utterly motionless.

I felt my power returning. My body worked furiously to heal me.

I could hear the soldiers who had attacked me shouting orders to one another as they made their way toward the back yard.

I got to my feet, slowly—painfully.

The soldiers were close. I could hear them opening the gate leading to the back yard. Leading to me.

I jumped into the air and flew away, leaving it all behind.

Chapter 17
Theories

I LIFTED THE DOOR to Samantha and Doug's storage unit and shut it behind me. I stumbled to the big comfortable chair and fell down into it. Then I slipped my hood off and sank deeper into the chair.

"That hurt," I said with a sigh.

"Looked like it," Samantha said from behind her desk.

I looked up and saw that Doug wasn't there. "Where's Doug?"

"He went home. He has school tomorrow."

I clenched my eyes shut and groaned. "So do I," I said, telling myself that more than Samantha.

"How are you feeling?" she asked, shutting her laptop.

"Not the best. Do you have any idea how bad that purple stuff hurts? It's not fun."

"I can imagine," she said, sitting back in her chair. "Looks like the government has another Super in their possession," she added, referring to Brian.

"Yeah, and he's my ex-girlfriend's current boyfriend, and he also bullied me my entire life until I knocked some screws loose. Now he's apparently the nicest guy ever."

"Geez, tonight just wasn't your night."

"Not at all." I sat up in my chair. "I'd better head home and try to get some rest before school tomorrow. What was that thing you wanted to tell me? Please say it has something to do with the government taking the Supers. I could really use some good news."

Samantha sighed and searched the corner of the room. "Well…it depends on how you look at it. Doug and I were going over all the profiles of the Supers so far. One thing we noticed is that they all seem to be under the age of twenty-five. I mean, we can't know for sure, but those that we do know about are, and from what we can guess from the others, they seem to be young."

"That's definitely interesting," I said, standing. "How do you know it's not just a coincidence, though?"

"It could be, but I doubt it. Twenty-five is the age when your brain is fully developed. We don't know what brain development has to do with all of it, but we think it has something to do with granting us our powers. We're just not sure exactly what yet."

I mulled over that information in my mind. So the key to our powers was in our brains, somehow. At least, that was what I had gathered from Samantha's theory. Although it was just that—a theory. Still, it was nice to have some sort of idea as to what was causing all of this. "I think we're on the right track," I said.

"Well, judging from the response time of that task force once Brian went all flaming, I'd say so," Samantha said with a satisfied smile.

"What do you mean?"

"I think the government is figuring all this out too, so

they're either putting people in schools and colleges to keep an eye out for Supers, or they're having students who are already there report any suspicious activity."

I thought back to the party tonight. I didn't remember seeing anybody there that I didn't recognize, but then again, I had a bit of a one-track mind. "I'm pretty sure it's the latter. I can't be a hundred percent sure, though."

"Well, in either case, keep an eye out. One thing's for sure, and it's that they've got their eye on Ebon High."

I nodded in agreement. This new development wasn't going to make my life any easier, that was for sure. "Speaking of which, I'd better get going. I've gotta think of some reason to tell Drew why I left without saying anything."

"Just say you left after your argument with Macy," Samantha said absentmindedly as she opened her laptop back up.

"What was that?" I asked. Had she been listening in on me?

Samantha stopped what she was doing, horror washing over her face. "I mean, I'm a girl, so if my ex showed up after being gone for six months, it could only end in an argument, right?"

I eyed her suspiciously. "Right."

"See? I'm pretty good at this girl thing," she said with a self-gratifying nod.

I rolled my eyes. "Good night, Samantha."

"Goodnight, Kane."

I left the storage unit and began flying home to Indianapolis.

Chapter 18
Speech Therapy

MORE RUMORS WERE spread the next day at school than the Monday after prom.

Everybody was talking about Brian and his superpowers. How long had he had them? Why had he used them at the party? Where had he gone?

The last one was the one that interested me the most. The official story was that he had been taken to the hospital and was recovering, but I knew that wasn't the case. I seemed to be the only one, though. Even people who'd been at the party—including Drew—believed Brian was lying in a hospital bed somewhere, making a speedy recovery. Everyone thought the soldiers in black had been there for Tempest, not Brian. I knew that, really, they were just trying to get two birds with one stone.

It almost worked, too. I couldn't stop thinking about how my powers had ceased to work for the few moments that the purple electricity was coursing through me. I was normal again. No longer Tempest, just Kane Andrews. It terrified me. I'd thought I had no weakness, but now I knew that that was no longer the case. And my biggest enemy knew that too.

As did the people whose house I'd crashed through, and the backyard I'd dug a hole in big enough for a new hot tub.

To make matters worse, that was Tempest's big return. Cell phone footage from the party had leaked, and was being played on the news 24/7. It was all people were talking about. After his six-month absence, Tempest had returned to stop a high school party.

Okay, so that's not exactly what happened. I did save who knows how many lives. Still, it wasn't the grand return I'd expected, or wanted. I wanted something grandiose. I wanted to let people know I was back, and I wasn't messing around.

The whole experience was definitely humbling. And it wasn't over, either.

Because I was sitting at the kitchen table in my apartment in Indianapolis, writing out the speech Samantha, Doug, and I were going to record that night and post on the internet.

I scribbled out the last sentence I'd written. Then the last paragraph. Then I just crumbled up the paper and threw it in the pile with the rest of the rejects.

"You know it's not going to be live. You can do more than one take," Mom said from the couch when she heard me groan in frustration.

"I know. I just want to have everything ready so I can get it over with. I gotta make sure it's perfect. There's going to be a lot of people who watch this," I said as I grabbed another piece of paper.

"Make sure you turn monetize the video. You can make a lot from YouTube ads," Mom said, only half-joking.

"I think that would make us pretty easy to track down," I said as I began writing.

"Speaking of which, I'd like to meet Samantha and Doug sometime. You should have them over for dinner."

"Mom, they live in California. They can't just fly over like I can."

"Yeah, well maybe—oh! You're on the news again!" Mom said, excited. She turned the television up.

I looked over my shoulder and saw myself on TV, telling everyone to back up and give Brian space. I barely recognized myself. My eyes were glowing bright, washing out most of my face. My suit was almost black from the fire, and parts of it were melted away. Muscles bulged from beneath the suit, but not excessively so. I didn't look like a bodybuilder or something, just really fit.

I thought about the six-pack I had, and couldn't help but smile. I'd always wanted one—or six—but I'd never thought they'd be a package deal with superpowers.

I looked at the clock and saw it was almost eight. I got up from the table and walked over to the closet that held my Tempest suits. "I gotta go, Mom. We're supposed to meet at six." Mom was about to say something about my being late, but I stopped her. "Time zones, Mom."

Mom smiled. "I was going to say good luck, and that I'm proud of you. You're doing the right thing, sweetheart."

I smiled back at her, and I genuinely felt a little bit less nervous about the whole ordeal. "Thanks, Mom." She'd come a long way from the way she'd acted when I first got my powers. Then, she was scared out of her mind, afraid for my life. But after what I'd been through, she knew that I could handle just about anything.

I put the Tempest suit on and felt the urge to tell Mom about what had happened with the government soldiers. I pushed those urges far down inside me. There was no way I could tell her. She would freak out—and with good reason. No, for now, I'd keep her in the dark.

I left the apartment wearing a coat over my suit. Once I got outside and into an alley, I slipped the Tempest hood over my face and then took off, flying toward Los Angeles.

*

"I brought some makeup. I used to apply it on the actors for the school play, so I know what I'm doing," Drew said as he reached into his backpack. He pulled out a handful of shades and began examining them, looking from my face to the selection before him. "Just gotta figure out your shade," he mumbled to himself.

"I think I'll be good without makeup," I said.

"Yeah, Doug, this isn't *Peter Pan*," Samantha said as she adjusted some settings on her camera. "Alright," she said as she put the camera on her tripod. "I think I've got everything where it needs to be."

I took a deep breath. We'd turned the storage unit into a mini movie studio—not the first time that'd been done in Los Angeles, I'm sure. Lights were strung up everywhere, and a white backdrop was taped up on the wall behind me.

I eyed the big comfortable chair that I normally sat in. We'd had to move it up against the entrance, and I really wanted to move it back and sit in it instead of standing. I felt so awkward just standing there. Plus the comfort of the chair would've calmed my nerves a little bit. However, just sitting in a chair addressing the camera seemed a little too maniacal; too Bond villain-ish. I might as well have sat down in a computer chair and spun around stroking a cat when the cameras started rolling. I chuckled at the thought of that. I'd probably name the cat Socks, because it would have black markings on its feet that would look like socks and—I shook the thoughts from my mind. I clenched my eyes and took a deep breath. *Focus, Kane. Focus,* I told myself. I was really, really nervous.

"You good?" Samantha asked.

I realized I'd been staring off into space, and came back to reality. "Yeah, yeah, I'm good. Just practicing in my head," I lied.

"Alright, well, we're going to do one really quick. You ready?"

I nodded.

"Okay." Samantha pushed a button on her camera. "Rolling."

Doug pressed a button on his audio recorder and held up his microphone. "Speed."

Speed? What the hell did that mean? Why were they speaking this lingo? I felt myself get lightheaded. I didn't know if I could do this.

"Can you give me a clap-sync?" Samantha said.

I looked at her like a deer in the headlights. A *what*?

"Just clap your hands so we can sync the sound," Samantha said with an eye roll.

I clapped my hands, feeling very, very stupid.

"Whenever you're ready."

I looked into the camera. My heart beat faster. Why was I so scared? I grew frustrated with myself. What was my problem? Why couldn't I just say anything? Why couldn't I own up to my mistakes?

I sighed.

I didn't know if I could do it. I didn't know if I could face the embarrassment of my failures. I thought about the bank in Dallas. How many people had I put out of a job that day?

How much money had that cost people? I was trying to be a hero, and I'd failed.

Now, I was trying to own up to my mistakes—to be a hero again. And I was failing miserably.

I looked to Samantha. "I don't kn—"

"Tempest," she said, stopping me. "I believe in you."

I was brought back to when I'd met Samantha in person for the very first time. She'd given me a hug and thanked me. She'd thanked me for stopping Richter. For saving the world. Like a hero would.

Suddenly, I didn't care what anybody thought about me. I didn't care what Holocene thought. I didn't care what Macy thought. I didn't care what the government thought.

I'd done my job. I'd stopped Richter. I was a hero. Everyone else could believe what they wanted, but that didn't change the fact that in Samantha's eyes, in my parents' eyes, and finally, in my own eyes, I was a hero.

I cleared my throat.

And the words flowed from my mouth.

"My name is Tempest. I have some things I need to get off my chest."

Chapter 19
Second Chances

MY SPEECH RACKED up a few million views in the first 24 hours after it was posted.

I couldn't help but think about how much I could've made from ad revenue, like Mom said.

It was all over the news, although every time it was on TV when I was in the room, I turned it off. I hated seeing myself on camera, even though you couldn't even recognize it was me.

Still, even though I couldn't help but cringe when it was on, I was proud of myself. I stood there and told everyone that I'd returned a little bit earlier then they'd thought, and that I was behind the bank collapsing in Dallas.

I didn't say where I'd been during those six months, however. I didn't want to add more fuel to the government's fire. If I told everyone they'd lied about the reasons behind refunding the shuttle program, it'd just add to the growing tension in the country. People were starting to get very upset that a teenager was doing more to protect them than the government—even though, really, they had no idea I was a teenager. If they knew that, there'd probably be chaos. People would be very, very, pissed.

My alarm went off, and I turned it off as soon as it did so. It was of no use to me this morning, since I had already been wide awake for a half hour. I'd enjoyed the peace and quiet for those thirty minutes. I'd been able to just lie there, lost in my own thoughts.

Now, however, it was time to get up. It was time to show people that Tempest was a hero—and hopefully, show Holocene that I was an ally.

It was a Saturday morning, Mom and Dad were still asleep. I put on my basketball shorts and t-shirt, then grabbed my latest Tempest outfit from my bedroom floor. I slipped it on, and then put on my jacket and sweatpants.

I left the apartment building, walked through my usual alley, and took off for Dallas.

I didn't go as fast as I could, but I wasn't taking my time either. I made a mental note to keep an eye out for Holocene. If she saw me flying around Dallas, she probably wouldn't be very happy, even if she'd seen my video. I hoped I'd be at the bank site before she saw me.

After a thirty-minute flight, I reached Dallas. I landed on top of a skyscraper downtown and shed my coat and sweatpants, revealing my Tempest outfit underneath. Even with the outfit and the clothes underneath, the cold wind bit at me. I could've used some of Brian's flames at that moment. Even though it was Texas, it still got pretty cold in December. Not Indiana cold, but still, nothing to sneeze at.

I made sure my clothes weren't anywhere where they'd blow away, and then flew to where the bank used to be. The construction crew was just arriving, working even on the weekend. They'd just begun to clean up the mess, and it would probably take a few solid days of work before they would be ready to move on to the next step.

Bulldozers picked at the rubble, piling it up. They would pick up a chunk, drop it in the back of a dump truck, and then go back to picking at their pile.

I smirked. I was about to give everybody the day off.

I flew down and began pushing everything into small piles. I then grabbed the pile and threw it in the back of one of the dump trucks. I filled up the first dump truck in fifteen seconds flat before moving on to the next one. In just a couple of minutes, the seven dump trucks that were lined up in the street had been filled to the brim with rubble, and a large part of the building had been cleaned up.

"You guys can go haul that off," I said to the truck drivers.

They all stared at me, their mouths open. They couldn't believe what they'd just seen. *The* Tempest, the guy who'd saved them from Richter just a few months ago, was now helping them do their jobs. It was like when a famous actor visited a hospital or one of his fans at work.

I mentally kicked myself. *Don't get cocky,* I thought. *Just do your job.*

"Tempest," a booming voice sounded from the sky.

I looked up and saw Holocene floating down to my eye level. "A word."

I looked down at the construction workers. They looked at each other, eyes wide. Then they pulled out their phones, their faces plastered with wonder. Two superheroes were about to have "a word".

Really, they should've been scared shitless.

Holocene turned and flew up to one of the skyscrapers.

I landed behind her, ready for her to berate me.

"I thought I told you not to come back here," she said. She crossed her arms as she turned to face me.

I shrugged. "I'm just trying to do my job. I made a mistake. I'm trying to do right by it."

"What's your angle?" she asked, narrowing her eyes.

"No angle, I swear," I said. I was telling the truth. I honestly just wanted to own up to my mistake. I wanted to be the hero everyone thought I already was.

"Okay, fine. You can do your little community service work. But I've got my eye on you, Tempest. Let's see if you can walk the walk."

With that, Holocene flew away, leaving me on top of the building.

I walked to the edge and looked out over the city of Dallas. I knew I could do it. I knew I had it in me. I could walk the walk.

More dump trucks pulled up, ready for me to load them. I flew down there and started doing what I'd come there to do: clean up after myself.

I started to work a little faster. I wanted to get everything done before news got out and the government showed up with their purple lightning guns. That was the last thing I needed.

Thankfully, that didn't happen. After thirty more minutes, the whole site was cleaned up, and they could start rebuilding ASAP.

I flew up to the skyscraper I'd left my belongings on and put on my clothes over my Tempest outfit. I heard someone land behind me, and whipped around.

"That was a good thing you did this morning. I'm impressed," Holocene said, looking me up and down with an approving smile.

I gave a facetious bow and smirked. “I’m glad the Queen of Dallas approves.”

Holocene glared at me, and I got the message that we weren’t on the “joking with each other” level yet.

“Look, you’re a step closer to me not trying to kill you anytime you set foot in my city. If you really want to prove you’re a hero, though, I could use your help with something.”

I was taken aback a bit, but recovered. “Yeah? What with?”

She hesitated. I could tell she wasn’t entirely sure about me, but she finally began to spill. “There’s a drug that started popping up here and there. It’s called Delvin. One of the ingredients is Super blood.”

“Shit, are you serious?” I asked. I couldn’t imagine what Super blood would do when mixed with a bunch of narcotics.

She nodded. “It’s giving people an extreme high, and they begin to hallucinate that they’re a Super, and have powers. The hallucinations are extremely realistic and addictive. Last night, I rescued a guy who thought he could fly and jump off the top of his apartment building. I was able to catch him, but it’s only a matter of time before people get themselves or others killed from it. If you want to win my trust, help me track down the Super who’s using his blood for this drug, and take him down.”

I thought about it for a moment. Delvin sounded like it was a very bad drug, and I was definitely up for taking it out. Besides, I’d be taking down a bad Super as well. That would definitely help my hero credibility, *and* get Holocene to trust me.

“Okay, you have a deal.”

Chapter 20

Enhanced Interrogation

"YOU SEE HIM?" Holocene asked me. We were floating high above downtown Dallas, unseen by all the people passing by below.

"Red hoodie, right?" I asked.

"Right."

I scanned the sparse crowd of people walking down the street until I found the guy. He was wearing a bright red hoodie, and was walking like someone was following him. He kept looking over his shoulder. If only he knew that the people who were after him were up above him, not behind him.

"Okay, I got him," I said. My eyes were locked on him. He wasn't leaving my sight.

"If what my contact says is true, he should be heading into an alley a couple of blocks ahead," Holocene said.

I nodded, my eyes still on the target.

He picked up his pace as if he knew he was being watched; he just couldn't figure out from where. He reached a crosswalk and jogged across the street, even though the pedestrian crossing sign was flashing an upheld hand, signaling it wasn't safe to cross.

"He's sure in a hurry," I said. "Are you sure we shouldn't just grab him now?"

"No, stick to the plan. We have to catch him red-handed, or else he'll just deny everything."

I was sure I could come up with a couple of ways for him to tell us what we wanted to know, but this was Holocene's plan. I had to follow her lead.

Our target reached an alley between an apartment building and an Indian restaurant, and disappeared between the two.

Holocene flew over to the space above the two buildings without saying a word. I followed close behind, my heart racing. I wasn't nervous because I thought we might be in danger, I was just afraid we weren't going to get from the man what we needed. My heart was also racing for another reason, and that was because I was excited to see how Holocene worked. I looked forward to learning a thing or two from her—maybe even *about* her. Even though my ego hated it, I had to admit that Holocene knew more about being a superhero then I did. Sure, I'd been the first one, but she'd been at the whole thing for a lot longer, and I had a lot to learn.

The man practically ran to a pile of moving boxes and pallets in the alleyway. He dug around in them until he found what he was looking for. He pulled out a red and black duffel bag and unzipped it, then pulled out the contents of the bag, and our suspicions were confirmed: inside the bag were many pouches of blood.

"Alright, I'll grab him," Holocene said.

Before I could respond, she had whipped down and grabbed the man by the back of his hoodie. She flew up toward the top of a skyscraper, zooming past me. The guy she'd grabbed hadn't even screamed. He was too busy trying to figure out what the hell was going on.

I flew up toward the building Holocene had disappeared on top of. I could hear the man's screams before I reached the top. I landed on the building and saw the man in the red hoodie backing away from Holocene as fast as he could, screaming for help.

"No one can hear you," she said calmly as she walked forward.

His gaze flashed to me, and his face dropped. "Please!" he shouted. He looked back and forth from me to Holocene. "Please don't hurt me!"

"Tell us what we want to know," Holocene said.

The man backed into the edge of the rooftop. He had nowhere to go but down. He looked over his shoulder and almost passed out. His entire face went white. He looked like he was about to need some of the blood he'd been carrying in that duffel bag.

"I'll tell you anything," he said, his voice weak.

Holocene looked over her shoulder at me. "You're up."

I nodded, ready for action. I remembered the questions she'd told me to ask. I stepped forward, and the man shrank down even more. I was a few feet away from him, trying to stand as tall as I could. His fearful eyes looked into my glowing ones. "Is the blood from a Super?"

"Y-yes. I don't know who, though, I swear! I was just supposed to pick it up and bring it down to Houston," he said as fast as he could.

"What's in Houston?"

"Rey Krev. He mixes the blood with his own concoction of drugs. Makes a new one. Calls it Delvin."

"Tell me something we don't already know!" Holocene yelled from behind me, sending the man into another wave of shaking and cowering.

"There's a shipment of supplies coming into port the day after tomorrow from China. It'll be at the Houston docks. That's all I know, I swear. I'm just someone trying to get by. Please don't kill me."

"We're not going to kill you," Holocene said. She walked over to the man and picked him up. He started screaming as loud as he could, pleading for his life.

Holocene jumped off the building, leaving me up there alone.

"Did you get that, Samantha?" I asked.

"Sure did. Doug is looking up all the ships coming into the Houston docks from China on Monday," she said in my head.

"Alright, good."

"Kane, isn't this all kinda petty? Don't we have bigger things to take care of, like the government kidnapping Supers, keeping an eye on the ones still out there, taking out the bad Supers, stuff like that?" Samantha asked for what seemed like the hundredth time.

"Samantha, this drug is the most powerful drug there is, and part of it is coming from a Super. A very bad Super. We *are* taking him down, and this will get Holocene on our side while we're at it. He's just very smart. He's not robbing banks, or destroying cities. He's staying hidden, in the dark. But don't worry, we should figure out everything we need to Monday night at the docks."

Holocene flew up and landed on top of the building. "Still talking to the voices in your head?" she asked with a smirk.

"Just filling Samantha in on a few things. Where's Mr. Hoodie?"

"Dropped him off at the police station. That was some good intel we got from him. You did some good work, too," she said, smiling.

"Well, it wasn't anything you couldn't have done on your own," I said.

"Yeah, but company's nice, and we don't all have voices in our heads."

"You're not wrong about that," I said with a chuckle. Samantha always having my back and being there to talk to was pretty sweet. "So, what next?"

"Meet me here Monday night. We'll fly down to Houston and be there when that shipment arrives. Someone will know who it's going to. If we can find them, we can find the Super behind all of this."

"Sounds good. I'll see you then."

I took off into the air, leaving Holocene and Dallas behind. As I flew back to Indianapolis, I couldn't help but feel like I was really becoming a hero.

Chapter 21
Shocking Revelations

MY PHONE BUZZED on the table next to my bed, waking me from my sleep. I picked it up and saw that it was Drew calling me.

"Hello?" I said into the phone.

"H-hey, Kane? You busy?" Drew asked. I could tell by the sound of his voice that something was wrong.

"No, man. I'm free. What's up? Is everything okay?" I asked, sitting up in my bed. I looked over at the clock and saw that it was nine-thirty in the morning.

"I just need to see you right now. Can you meet me behind the home bleachers at the football field?"

I cocked my head to the side, taken aback by Drew's strange request. "Are you sure? You don't want to meet at the Burger Shack or something?"

"No! I-uh-no. Sorry, I just gotta show you something."

"Okay, I'll be there in fifteen," I said.

"Thanks, I appreciate it," Drew said. He hung up.

I sat in bed for a moment, playing over the conversation we'd just had in my head. What could Drew possibly want to show me that he had to do it in such a weird location? From the sound of his voice, it wasn't anything good. Drew had sounded afraid—an emotion I wasn't one hundred percent sure he knew until just now.

I could get to the bleachers behind the school in less than a minute, so after getting ready, I spent the next twelve minutes pacing around my room, trying to figure out what could be going on.

Once it was time, I raced outside—maybe a little *too* fast—entered my alleyway, and took off flying toward Ebon High School.

I landed behind some trees near the school and began walking toward the bleachers of the football field. Using my super vision, I could see Drew pacing back and forth underneath the seats, waiting for me. I picked up the pace a little bit and reached the bleachers in no time.

"Thanks for coming, Kane," he said when he saw me.

I gave him a fist bump. "What's going on? Why'd you want to meet here?"

"Something crazy's happening, and I don't know what to do. I couldn't meet you at home because my parents would freak out."

"What is it?"

"Well, when those guys rolled up at Zach's party and started shooting those purple electricity bolts at Tempest?" Drew began. Already I didn't like where this was going.

I nodded. "Yeah, I remember hearing about those."

"Well, one of them nicked me. It wasn't a direct hit, but it was enough to make my hair stand up, that's for sure."

"Jesus," I exclaimed. "Are you alright? It didn't hurt you, did it?"

"I'm standing here, aren't I?"

"You know what I mean. Did you get any help?"

He shook his head. "Everybody was freaking out about Tempest, and then the house on fire, shit like that. Besides, the pain went away almost instantly. I was perfectly fine—or so I thought." Drew looked around, making sure nobody was spying on us. "This is why I wanted to meet you here." Drew rolled up the sleeves on his shirt. His arms were covered in white scars. They looked as if they were roots from a tree spreading from his fingertips all the way up his arms and disappearing into his sleeves.

I couldn't believe my eyes. It looked incredible. Like some sort of elaborate tattoo done with white ink. "Holy shit, Drew," I began, but I couldn't find any more words. My mouth hung open and I found myself unable to look away.

"They showed up this morning, right after I did this for the first time." Drew thrust his arms out at his sides, and they exploded with purple lightning. It coursed up and down his arms, crackling and popping. The sudden electricity caused my hair to stand on end. The whole underneath of the bleachers lit up purple, the faint shadows dancing all around to the rhythm of the lighting that pulsed up and down Drew's arms.

"Oh my god," was all I could whisper.

Drew stood there smiling at me. "I think I'm one of the Supers," he said with a laugh.

My heart raced and my knees felt week. It sure looked like he was one. His eyes weren't glowing like those of most of the other Supers did, but I couldn't deny the fact that purple electricity was dancing up and down on his body.

I found myself taking a small step back. If it was the same type of electricity that the government agents shot from their guns, one zap would send me into convulsions, taking away my powers until I could recover.

"Is that all you can do?" I asked.

"So far. Who knows if I'll get anything else?" Drew stopped the electricity, and I held back a sigh of relief. The air felt crisp and smelled burnt as the electricity lingered in the air.

"That's crazy, man," I said, trying to act as excited as I could. My eyes lingered on his arms. Just underneath his skin was the electricity that took away my powers. That made me feel pain. That terrified me. "What are you going to do about it?"

"I don't know. I'm still kinda freaked out by it all. I just wanted you to know about it," he said with a weak smile.

I thought I was going to be sick. Guilt washed over me. I was the first person he had told after he got his powers. I'd been Tempest for months, and had never said a word. I wasn't sure if I was being smart, or Drew was being stupid.

"Kane, we've got a very bad situation with a Super in Chicago," Samantha said in my head.

I felt my pocket, like my phone was vibrating. I retrieved it and looked at the screen, making sure Drew couldn't see. "Oh, dammit, my mom's calling. I gotta take this."

Drew nodded. "No problem."

I swiped across the screen, and put the phone up to my ear. "Hey, I'm with Drew. What's up?"

"There's a Super who just showed up in Chicago. He's in the middle of a standoff with the police. He's a teleporter, and is just toying with them. Once he gets tired, though, he could take them all out easily," Samantha said in a panic.

"Okay, yeah. I gotcha. I'll be right there." I slipped my phone back into my pocket.

Drew raised his eyebrows, curious as to what was going on.

"Yikes. Mom went into my room. Didn't like the mess she saw. She said I had to get home or else I'm grounded," I said, taking a step back.

"Can't you stay a little little longer? I have some stuff I wanna talk about."

"Yeah, sorry, bro, I really can't. Mom's been on a tear lately. She means business. I could be grounded for a month if I don't get back ASAP."

Drew nodded, but his face grew long. "Yeah, okay. I understand."

"I'll text you as soon as I can," I said as I backed out from underneath the bleachers.

"Okay, thanks for coming."

"Anytime," I said. "See ya." I turned and ran toward the parking lot. As soon as Drew was out of my line of sight, I took off into the air. "Samantha, can you get Holocene? I could use her help," I said once I was in the air.

"I don't think she'd appreciate my voice in her head," Samantha argued.

"Samantha, come on. This will help get her on our side faster."

"Fine. I'll see if I can get her."

"Thanks. Tell her to meet me on top of our usual building."

"Okay, but be quick about it. No telling when this guy's gonna snap."

Chapter 22

Standoff

I LANDED ON THE rooftop in Dallas seconds before Holocene did. I barely had time to pull the Tempest hood over my head before she landed.

"Tell your friend to stay out of my head," Holocene said, her voice filled with venom.

"I'll be sure to relay the message," I said. "Look, there's a guy who can teleport who's playing around with the police up in Chicago. I could use your help."

"How do you know you need me? The great Tempest can't do it on his own?" Holocene asked with a smirk, clearly enjoying the fact that I was asking for her help.

I sighed. "Look, the last time I went into a situation thinking I had it under control, it went poorly. I'm just trying to keep my ego in check. I may be overcompensating, but whatever. You in or not?"

Holocene nodded. "Yeah, I'm in."

"Race you to Chicago," I said with a smile. I launched into the air, flying as fast as I could to the Windy City, Holocene hot on my tail.

We reached Chicago in no time. We came to a stop over the Sears Tower and scanned the area.

"There, I see the police cars," Holocene said, pointing to where the standoff was taking place. Police and SWAT cars surrounded a construction site where new apartment buildings were being built.

There was a flash of light behind one of the officers, and a man so pale he was almost white appeared. His head was shaved, and an evil smirk marked his face. He grabbed an officer and the two of them disappeared in another flash.

I looked around, trying to see where the two of them had gone. I heard the officer scream and searched for the source of the sound. I saw the teleport holding the officer over the edge of the building. With a laugh, the man let go, and the officer fell. He screamed and writhed in the air, and I flew into action.

I reached the police officer and grabbed him by his bulletproof vest. I slowed his descent as fast as I could until he came to a stop just a few feet from the ground. Then I flew him behind the line of officers and turned my attention up to the teleport.

A gunshot sounded in the air, and an explosion of blood shot from the teleport's chest. Seconds later, Holocene appeared from behind him and kicked him off the building.

I prepared to jump up to catch him, but the man teleported. He appeared inches above Holocene and came crashing down on her.

I jumped up onto the flat roof of the building just as he was standing. He didn't seem to be injured. In fact, the hole in his chest where the bullet had entered was sealed up. Great. He was a teleport, *and* he could regenerate.

I dashed to him and swung at his face. Not as hard as I

could, but knowing he could regenerate, harder than a normal human could probably take.

Right before my punch connected, he teleported with a flash. I stumbled over myself, the momentum from my punch not landing causing me to stumble forward.

I turned and saw the man standing there with a huge smile.

"The breeze from you missing felt quite nice," he said with a thick Russian accent.

I gritted my teeth and swung for him again. He teleported away, but Holocene was ready for him when he appeared to my right. She swung at him before he was ready, and her punch connected.

The man flew back a few feet, skidding across the rooftop. I dashed to him and grabbed the back of his shirt, about to throw him to the ground. Before I could, there was a flash, and I felt dizzy and disoriented.

Suddenly I was standing on the sidewalk outside of the new apartment buildings. The man grabbed my outfit and threw me over him. Right before he let go of me, he teleported me into the middle of a highway somewhere in Chicago, right in front of a semi truck.

The truck hit me with extreme force, sending pain shooting through my body. I felt my bones snap and the popping sensation as they began to repair themselves. The front of the truck had been crushed; I could feel the metal and steel crumple beneath me.

The truck flipped forward, and my instincts kicked in before I fully realized what was going on. I pushed myself out of the grill of the truck and reached through the hole where the windshield had been as the truck flipped over me. I yanked the seatbelt off the truck driver and pulled him out of the cab, then pulled him close and ducked to the ground, shielding his body with mine.

The truck and the trailer it had been pulling landed just a few feet behind the two of us with a deafening crash. It screeched as it slid across the ground before finally coming to a stop.

I stood up and inspected the truck driver. “You okay?” I asked.

He just looked at me, his eyes wide. He was clearly shell-shocked. I grabbed him and ran to the side of the road, then set him down.

“Stay here. Help will come,” I told him.

He nodded. His gaze wandered to the crumpled mess that had once been his big rig.

I jumped into the air and scanned the area. Just a couple of blocks away, I saw Holocene fighting the teleport on the roof. She was learning to anticipate where he would be, and was able to get a couple of shots in.

I flew toward him, my fist in front of me. I was ready to end this. I gritted my teeth and prepared to hit him as hard as I thought I could without shattering him into a million pieces.

He never saw me coming. My fist slammed into his back. I felt his spine snap beneath my fist, and the two of us fell through the roof.

We fell through the fourth floor. I kept applying pressure.

The third. He slammed his head on a bathtub.

The second. I began to slow down and let the teleport’s own momentum carry him.

The first. He slammed into the floor, causing a small crater to form and cracks to web out from the point of impact.

I landed next to him and picked him up. He was a rag

doll in my hands, his body bloody and broken. I could feel his bones cracking and popping into place as his body tried to repair itself as fast as it could. I could tell his regeneration wasn't as fast as mine, though. I'd already have been ready to fight back.

There was a flash, and he disappeared from my hands. Maybe I was wrong.

I jumped up through the holes I'd made with the teleport's body and landed on the roof. When I looked down to the street, I saw him crawling away from the building toward the police officer.

"Help me!" he screamed. He got up to his knees and inched forward on them. "Please, I need help!" he pleaded with the officers.

They stood there and watched as the man who had terrorized them struggled to stand.

He stumbled to his feet and took a few steps forward.

The officers raised their guns. "Stop right there!" they screamed.

"Plea—"

A purple bolt of electricity came out of nowhere and hit the teleport.

I jumped back, startled. I looked behind the officers and saw that the soldiers cloaked in black had appeared from behind the front lines.

I took a step forward, about to go take care of them, but Holocene put a hand on my chest, stopping me. "Let's just get out of here," she said. She took off into the air before I could protest.

I had no choice but to follow her. We flew away, leaving Chicago behind, and our latest enemy in the hands of another.

Chapter 23

Heavy Silence

I WALKED INTO THE living room after my hot shower, and couldn't help but smile when I saw what was on TV. The news was covering my and Holocene's team-up, especially how I'd saved that police officer from hitting the ground. They were speculating that I'd been involved in the eighteen-wheeler crash, too.

The mysterious government soldiers coming and taking the teleport away was suspiciously absent from their report, however.

"Looks like you were busy," Dad said when he saw I was standing there.

I smirked. "It's been a crazy day, that's for sure." I thought back to earlier in the morning and Drew's revelation to me.

"What're your plans? You up for some bowling later, once your mom gets back from the store?" he asked. He turned off the TV and stood up from the couch.

"Maybe not right when she gets back. I gotta run to LA and talk over some things with Samantha and Doug. I'll be back around five, though," I said as I walked over to the door.

"Okay, that sounds good to me. We'll throw in some dinner and make a night of it."

I opened the door. "I like the sound of that. See you later, Dad." I shut the door behind me, and in a few minutes, the Hollywood sign was already in my sights.

*

"Got you a double with no onions," Doug said as I entered the storage unit that he and Samantha had set up shop in.

I grabbed the bag that had my food in it and sat down in my big comfy chair. Samantha passed me my drink. "Thank guys," I said.

"No problem. Looked like you could use it after what happened in Chicago," Samantha said after swallowing a bite of her burger.

I sighed as I chewed my food. "That guy was a quick thinker," I said after swallowing. "I'd be okay with never seeing him again."

"Well, after those government guys showed up and took him away, you'll probably have your wish granted," Samantha said.

"How'd you know about that? The news wasn't reporting it," I said.

"I was watching the whole thing," she said, tapping on her temple.

"Right, forgot about that. I was kinda distracted."

Doug laughed. "Yeah, sure seemed like it. I would be too if I was getting sweaty and wrestling with Holocene."

My cheeks flushed. I hadn't expected something so overt and direct from Doug, especially since that wasn't the case at all.

"The hell are you talking about?" Samantha snapped at him. She looked at him like he was truly the stupidest person ever.

He shrugged as he took another bite of his burger. "Just saying."

"We weren't even fighting each other," I said. "That made no sense."

Doug put his hands up in defense. "Just a jo—oh. You're right."

I looked over at Samantha and saw she was concentrating on Doug. "You just told him something, didn't you?"

Samantha was visibly angry with Doug. She shot him daggers from her eyes. "You're an idiot."

Doug smiled, showing his teeth and the bits of food stuck between them.

"Sorry, I was just saying that given certain recent events regarding females, now probably wasn't the best time to bring up Holocene," Samantha explained.

Oh, right. Macy. I wouldn't even have thought of her had Samantha not brought her up. I felt my stomach twist, and my appetite left with my next breath.

My thoughts turned to Drew, and I remembered the whole reason I had stopped by. "So I've found another Super, and I don't think he's on any of you guys' radars."

This piqued Doug and Samantha's interest, and they both suddenly forgot all about the awkward exchange we'd just had.

I explained to them everything that had happened with Drew that morning, leaving out no detail. I even told them how I was afraid of him, and what his powers could do to me. At least, what I assumed they could do. I realized that I wasn't even one hundred percent sure. Just ninety-five percent, which was close enough for me.

"Maybe the graze from the bolt he experienced messed with the neurons in his brain. At least, that's what we think it does to Supers," Samantha said.

"What exactly do you think it does to us?" I asked.

"Just a theory, but I think the core of our powers is in our brains. They've figured out some way to block, or fry, or scramble, or do *something* to our brains when we're hit with the lightning."

I thought back to when I was hit by one of the bolts. "That makes sense. I felt as if my head was going to explode when I got hit by one."

"Yeah, I think it's a pretty solid theory. I wish I could learn more about it, though. It might help us learn more about where our powers come from."

"Well, I guess that means the government knows more about our powers than we do, if they were able to develop something like this, and that's *very* unsettling to think about," I said, leaning back in my chair.

That thought lingered in the air as the three of us sat in silence. We were all lost in thinking about what the government could be doing with all the Supers they were gathering. The types of things they were learning.

"Are you going to bring Drew in?" Samantha asked.

Broken from my train of thought, I turned to her. "What do you mean?"

"Are you going to tell him about you? About all of this?" Samantha asked, gesturing to the room around us.

"I don't know. I haven't had much time to think about it. I don't know what his reaction would be. I was the first one he told about his powers, and he still has no idea about mine," I said.

"To be fair, when you got yours it was kind of an urgent situation. You didn't have much time to show off to all of your friends. Then you were out in space for six months, so you can always just say you didn't have the time," Samantha offered.

I sighed. "Yeah, but this is something I should've made the time for."

Once again, we all sat in silence.

"I know what the right thing to do would be," I said. "But I don't know if I could do it. It would probably mean losing Drew as a friend."

"Telling him or not, that's still a possibility," Samantha said, saying what I hated to hear.

"That's the crux of this situation." I stood up. "I need to think. I'll talk to you guys tomorrow. Get some rest tonight, because tomorrow's when Holocene and I are going to the docks." I felt the answer pop into my head—or the best excuse, at least. "Once that's taken care of, we'll focus on the Drew situation."

"Sounds good," Samantha said. "Talk to you tomorrow."

Chapter 24

The Docks

AT SCHOOL THE next day, the Drew situation wasn't a factor, as Drew was absent. This worried me, as I was worried what he was up to. However, deep down I was relieved that our confrontation—however it went—was postponed.

My thoughts turned to the shipment coming into the docks in Houston that night, and how Holocene and I would be there waiting for it to arrive. I enjoyed working with her, and was glad she was becoming an ally. She was a powerful one, and I felt sorry for anyone who might underestimate her.

I wondered what her real name was. Who the *real* Holocene was. Was she my age? Was she sitting in a boring high school class thinking the same about me? Or was she out of high school, and like Samantha, focused only on the Supers? I hoped that I could at least find out the answer to one of those questions soon. I'd be satisfied if I could find out what her first name was, mostly because that would mean she trusted me. That in her eyes I was a hero.

*

Holocene and I floated above the Houston docks and watched

as armed guards stood around an eighteen-wheeler as workers loaded the contents of one of the shipping containers into the trailer.

"What's the plan?" I asked her. "Do we tail the truck and see where it takes us?"

"The fastest way from here to Dallas is north on I-45, and that will take hours. I don't have the patience for that. We're going to do this the quick and easy way."

I wasn't sure I liked the sound of that. "And what exactly is that?"

Holocene flashed me a smile. "Asking the driver nicely. I'll grab him and get what we need to know. You make sure those guards aren't going anywhere, and take care of all those drugs," she said.

I looked down at the scene below us. There were about a dozen guards and a truckload of drugs. I wasn't sure why they didn't just load the shipping container onto the truck bed and take the whole thing to Dallas, instead of having to deal with transferring everything between it and the truck trailer. It didn't change the fact that that's what was happening, though, and I began to put together a plan in my head.

"You ready for this?" Holocene asked me.

I nodded and smiled. "Ladies first."

She rolled her eyes as they began to glow, but still smirked at me. She disappeared in a blur and grabbed the driver.

I turned on the glow in my eyes and flew down, landing on top of the shipping container. The steel bent beneath my feet and the thud echoed throughout the shipping yard.

Yelps of surprise sounded from the guards, but that was replaced by the clicking of their guns as they them trained on me, safeties off.

I smiled. This felt good. I was in my element. Thirteen heartbeats filled my ears. Twelve of them were fast and erratic, one of them calm and smooth.

Guess which one was mine.

I jumped down from the container, and twelve machine guns went off. I ran away well before the bullets could reach me. I jumped on top of the trailer of the eighteen-wheeler and watched as the bullets entered the container and ripped apart the drugs still inside.

White powder filled the air, as well as the sounds of glass shattering and liquids spilling on the ground.

"Nice! I'm guessing you all did that on purpose? You learning your lesson?" I shouted down from the top of the trailer.

They all jumped, realizing I was no longer in front of them. They searched around frantically, trying to figure out where I'd gone. They saw me on top of the eighteen-wheeler trailer and trained their guns on me. A couple of them fired off shots, but I dodged them with ease.

"Excuse me. I need to take care of something," I told them.

I jumped down from the trailer and grabbed the storage container. I picked it up with ease, even though it weighed tons. I spun in the air, gaining momentum, thenlet go of the container, sending it flying out to the ocean. I watched it until it eventually disappeared over the horizon.

Return to sender, I thought. I wanted to say that out loud, but I stopped myself. That would be too much.

I turned around and saw the twelve guards staring at me, practically shitting their pants.

"Alright, guys. Everybody drop your guns and get into the back of the eighteen-wheeler."

Twelve sets of eyes stared up at me, dumbfounded.

"*Now!*" I screamed, projecting my voice.

They threw their guns to the ground, and were almost fighting each other to be the first ones into the trailer. I snapped their guns in half and then carefully picked up the trailer.

I flew softly and steadily, doing my best to not rock the trailer back and forth. I found a nearby police station and brought the trailer down in the parking lot. I set it down gently and opened the back doors.

"Alright, everybody, let's go. Time to turn yourselves in."

The guards climbed out and stood outside the trailer. When they looked up at me I thumbed toward the station doors.

"I'm trying to be nice here. I'm trying not to hurt anybody." The tone of my voice changed. "Don't test me."

They began walking toward the station doors.

Holocene flew down and they started running, afraid of what two Supers might do. She dropped off the driver. "Go, join your friends," she said as she set the man down.

The man fell to the ground, stumbled to his feet, and took off running toward the police station.

"From what I saw, that was very entertaining," Holocene said with a grin.

I shrugged. "Just trying to have a little fun. I've used my fists a lot lately. It's nice to not have to."

"Well, the night's still young. I've got what I need to know. They were taking the supplies to a nightclub in Dallas called Purple Venus. Apparently the owner is known for his incredible strength and his generosity when it comes to blood donations."

"Sounds like our guy," I said as I began rising into the air.

Holocene rose with me, ready to take off. "Sounds like it. I think you might need your fists for this one, though."

I popped my knuckles. "I'm warmed up and ready to go."

"Race you to Dallas."

Chapter 25
Purple Venus

DESPITE HOLOCENE SAYING that the night was still young, by the time we got to Purple Venus, it was young no longer. We decided to wait until it was past 2 a.m. so that any patrons of the nightclub would be gone and it would be just us and Bruce Culver, the owner of the nightclub.

I was hoping that I could use the couple of hours we had to kill to learn more about Holocene, but she said she had to take care of some things and that she would meet me in our usual spot in downtown Dallas.

So by the time the two of us were standing in front of the doors of Purple Venus in Deep Ellum, I still was none the wiser about who Holocene really was.

We marched up the steps, Holocene in the lead. She kicked open the doors to the club, and there, standing in the middle of the dance floor, was Bruce, waiting for us.

The main fluorescent lights were on instead of the party lights, so you could really see how dirty and nasty the club Bruce was standing in the middle of really was.

Bruce looked at us, flashing a dirty, toothy smile. "Nice to meet you," he said.

I looked at Holocene, confused. Bruce didn't look like a Super. All the Supers so far were under the age of 25, and Bruce looked to be way older.

"So you're the guy who makes Delvin?" Holocene said, taking a step forward.

"That's right," Bruce said. But that was it. Nothing more, nothing less. I could hear his heart beating faster and could see sweat dripping from his hands.

"Samantha," I said as quietly as I could. "Tell Holocene something's wrong." Bruce was nervous. Too nervous. I didn't like this one bit.

"Are you going to let us take you in the easy way or the hard way?" Holocene asked, getting into her fighting stance.

I looked closely and saw something in Bruce's ear. An earpiece to a walkie-talkie.

Holocene turned and looked at me, her eyes questioning. I looked over her shoulder and saw Bruce give a slight nod.

I could hear soldiers stomping up the stairs behind us.

"Holocene, run!" I yelled.

Holocene saw the soldiers coming over my shoulder, and leapt into the air. They fired a flurry of purple lightning bolts into the room, and I jumped out of the way.

One of the bolts clipped Holocene as she launched herself through the ceiling, sending her flying, of course, disappearing into the night.

I jumped up into the air, ready to fly after her and escape, but before I could, a searing pain hit my calf and I fell to the ground.

Electricity coursed through my brain as two more bolts hit me dead on. I felt more and more crash into me within a matter of seconds, and before I knew it, I found myself slipping into unconsciousness.

Chapter 26

The Name of a Hero

MY EYES FLUTTERED open. Light flooded into my vision, and I squeezed them tight. My head pounded and buzzed, like bees were flying around in my skull, stinging as they did so.

"Hello, Tempest," a voice said.

I cracked my eyes open and my vision adjusted. A bright light sat above me, shining directly on me. My eyes adjusted more and I saw I was in a dark room, sitting on a metal chair. My hands were restrained to the armrests rests of the chair by a silver band that went across my wrists and another just below my shoulder. Similar bands wrapped across my ankles and above my kneecaps. The only source of light was one shining directly on me.

"Are you comfortable?" the voice said, clearly amused.

I looked to its source and recognized the face of the government woman I'd worked with months ago during the Richter crisis. "Agent Loren?"

"It's Director Loren now," she corrected me. Her once long black hair was now cut into a bob. Her eyes looked tired and worn from months of intense stress. "Director Loren of the STF—the Super Task Force."

"So you're behind the all the Supers disappearing," I said, my voice weak. I licked my dry lips, but my tongue offered little saliva to soothe my sore, cracked skin.

"That we are. And soon we'll be known as the ones behind the eradication of the Supers," she said with a sly smile.

I yanked on my restraints. I'd show her that it wasn't going to be that easy. But when I jerked, the metal bands didn't come flying off. I wasn't suddenly free, bursting through the roof to freedom. I yanked some more, the panic within me increasing. What was going on? Why weren't these bands as fragile as tinfoil?

"Having trouble?" she asked.

"What did you do?" I screamed.

Loren laughed, and teased, "Come on, Tempest. You can do it."

I grew tired from the struggle. I stopped to catch my breath, trying to hold back the panic that threatened to explode inside me.

"I simply brought you down to our level. *Beneath* our level," Loren said with a satisfied smirk. She took a step toward me. Her face blocked the light, silhouetting her figure. "Do you feel a buzzing in your head? Can you feel the static?"

I didn't answer. I stared into her eyes, trying my best to remain as stone-cold as I could be. But I was slipping.

"We've implanted a device beneath the skin in your neck, attached to your spine. It's constantly putting out a low charge of what we like to call Eximus energy. You're familiar with the Eximus, when it takes the form of purple lightning. It's blocking certain receptors in your brain that are part of what provides you with your powers." She took a step back and pulled a device from her pocket. "In fact, I can control how much energy you're receiving." She tapped on her screen. "A little."

I felt the static receding. My thoughts were becoming clearer and I felt my strength returning. I pulled up on the bands and felt them bending from the force. I was almost free.

"Or a lot."

The Eximus shot through my head in powerful waves. I screamed in pain as the electricity coursed up from the back of my neck and into my brain. All my strength left, replaced by utter weakness. I didn't even have the strength to think. Just scream.

The pain receded and the waves decreased from a tsunami to small breakers.

"What I'm trying to say, Tempest, is that I hold the power," Loren said as she slipped the device back into her pocket. "Why don't we get started with a few questions, shall we?" she said, her tone changing as if she were giving an interview for employment. "Let's start simple: what is your name?"

I looked at Loren, a weak smile growing across my face, and let out a small chuckle. "Really? That's your first question?"

"We're just trying to get a baseline. Something simple to make sure the Eximus isn't messing with your brain in ways we don't want it to," Loren said. Her expression turned dark. "Your name."

Since when did the government care about what the Eximus did to my brain? It was already messing with it in ways that terrified me. They seemed not to care at all what their invention did to Supers. "John Doe," I said with a smile.

Loren reached into her pocket and without looking, dialed up the dosage of Eximus.

My whole body went rigid as it seized with pain. The electricity coursed through me for a split second before it was dialed down. My breathing was fast and weak. I wasn't sure how much of this I could take.

"Tempest, your name," she said, her frustration growing.

It was fun seeing Director Loren getting upset, especially since I was the cause of it. In my own passive-aggressive way, I currently had the upper hand. "My name is Neil Armstrong."

Loren bumped up the Eximus again, sending another torrent of pain and misery my way.

"I could do this all day, Tempest. I quite enjoy this," Loren said. I could tell she wasn't lying about enjoying torturing me, but her anger and frustration at me for not correctly answering her question mounted. Her right hand was squeezed tight in a fist at her side, while the other was in the pocket of her coat, ready to turn up the voltage once again.

"Okay, okay," I said. I was trying to hold back a laugh. "My name is George Lucas. I was kidnapped by Tom Cruise a—" A hit of Eximus interrupted me, filling my body with pain. I couldn't speak, but my joke mixed with the frustration I was causing Loren caused me to laugh. I laughed uproariously through the pain. If I could see myself at that moment, I was sure I'd look like a madman. And maybe I was one.

"It's a simple question, Tempest. What is your name?"

The answer hit me and I found myself laughing even harder. "You don't know, do you?" Hearing myself say the words caused more fits of laughter to rush through me, followed by waves of the Eximus. "You don't know!" I screamed.

Director Loren let out a grunt in frustration and stormed

out of the room, slamming the door behind her. I continued laughing, turning my laughter partly into screams, hoping the sound would follow Loren down the hallway. I imagined the sound of my laughter following her down the halls, haunting her.

I settled down and chuckled to myself. "They don't even know my name," I mumbled. Another chuckle escaped my mouth. But then it hit me. I stared at the ground, confused. "How the hell do they not know my name?"

I'd been in their possession for who knew how long. I didn't have my powers. I had no way to fight back. How had they not taken blood samples, hair samples, pictures, fingerprints, every bit of identifying information they could take from me and run it through the government database? How did they not already know everything about me, my friends, family, where I lived, went to school—everything?

Something wasn't right, and it was more than just the fact that I'd been captured and didn't have my powers.

CHAPTER 27

NOT FINISHED WELCOME TO THE STF

I LOOKED DOWN AT the grey shirt I was wearing. Across the front in big black letters was the word TEMPEST. Below it was the insignia of STF, a ***insert here***.

It might as well have been a bull's-eye.

I looked across the commons room. There were three lines of tables, some couches in a corner, a bookshelf filled with the latest books along with some classics, and a TV with game systems hooked up to it. I looked up at the high ceiling where large stage lights were hung. In a ring around the ceiling were glass windows, behind which scientists were taking notes on clipboards, monitoring readings on computers and watching us like the lab rats they saw us as.

I scanned the room and searched for anybody that I recognized. Specifically, I searched for Brian. He was about to find out who I was. It was inevitable. I just wanted to get to him before he was able to shout my name. He had to know that he had to pretend he had no idea who I was. If he gave my identity away, I'd lose what little leverage I had over Loren and the STF.

“Holy. Shit,” someone said. It was someone sitting at the table closest to me, a young boy with dark skin. His shirt didn’t have a name on it like mine; his simply had the numbers *10927* printed across the front.

He stood from his seat. The people around him stopped what they were doing and looked at him, trying to figure out what was going on. They followed his gaze, and it led straight to me.

Soon, the whole room was looking at me. Staring. Reading the name on my shirt and then dropping their jaws. It was like clockwork.

I stood there awkwardly, not sure what to do. Everybody was just staring at me. It was like they were waiting for me to start flying around the room. To burst a hole through the roof and lead everyone to freedom. It was miserable. I could feel the eyes of the scientists watching me from behind the glass up above. I wanted to rip my shirt off and tear it to shreds. I wanted to say it was a joke, that I wasn’t really Tempest. This was just some sort of test.

Instead, I finally walked over to a water fountain nearby and got a drink. I heard whispers behind me as people began to speculate what I was doing there.

“Well, shit,” I heard someone say. “I was counting on him to save us. Now I’m gonna die here.”

“You think he’s strong enough to overpower the Eximus?”

“I thought he was working with the government the whole time.”

“You son of a bitch.”

I turned around after the last one and saw Brian Turner standing inches away from me. His face was red with anger. He looked like a bull that was about to charge.

I walked past him, toward a guy with large round glasses and shaggy brown hair. He was drawing something on the pages of a notebook.

"Hey, I'm talking to you!" Brian yelled after me. People were starting to turn their attention back to me. I needed to act fast.

I ripped a piece of paper from the notebook.

"Hey, what the—oh, shit." His face went white when he saw the name on my shirt.

"Can I borrow your pen?" I asked. I looked over my shoulder and saw Brian sauntering over toward the two of us. I had a feeling things were about to escalate very quickly. And I didn't have my powers to help me.

The guy with the glasses stumbled over his words, not sure how to respond. I grabbed the pen from his hands. "Thanks," I said as I started writing.

Identity secret. They'll go after Macy.

I thrust the paper into Brian's chest when he reached me. He grabbed it and was about to throw it aside when something caught his eye.

He gave me a disgusted look and shoved the paper at me. "Watch your back, *Tempest*."

I breathed a sigh of relief and handed the pen back to the guy. "Thanks again…?"

"Hank."

"Thanks, Hank. I appreciate it."

I realized everyone was still watching me. I looked around, and wherever my gaze went, people averted their eyes. Everybody pretended that nothing was up and that it was just a regular day.

I looked down at the piece of paper in my hands. It was

incriminating, to say the least. Brian's confrontation could be explained away as someone who didn't like Tempest confronting him, but if they saw what was on the note, they'd know that the two of us were connected.

I tore the small section of paper that I'd written on off the rest of the sheet and crumpled it up into as small of a ball I could. Then I tossed the ball of paper into my mouth. I gave it a good hard swallow and the little ball of paper went down.

"Huh," Hank said.

I opened my eyes and looked down. Hank was sitting there staring up at me.

I chuckled nervously. "Oh, uh, sorry about that."

"Don't worry, we all need our fiber," Hank said, returning to his drawing. I noticed his hand was shaking and he was trying desperately not to call attention to it.

I sat down across from him. He looked at me over the top of his glasses and went back to drawing, trying to ignore me.

"So, Hank, any pointers?" I asked, trying to start a conversation. It felt awkward and forced, but I didn't want to just sit in the corner feeling everyone staring at the name printed across my chest. I wanted to at least try to fit in.

"Well, if I were going to give anybody else any pointers, it'd be to not hang around with the most hated guy in the room," Hank said, not looking up from his paper.

I laughed nervously. "I guess my reputation precedes me?"

Hank frowned. "Most of the people here aren't one of the good guys like you. The good guys are better at not getting caught, usually because they're not the ones trying to rob banks. Some of the guys are even here because of you—or at least that's the way they see it. Hate and fear make more noise than anything."

"So which one are you?" I asked.

Hank frowned again. This time he looked puzzled. "I'm sorry?"

"What are you? One of the good guys, or one of the others?"

"I'm just a sixteen-year-old kid who's trying to draw."

I moved around in my seat, repositioning myself so I could see what Hank was drawing. I opened my mouth to ask him a question, but what came out was a yelp of surprise.

I was pulled backwards from my seat and thrown to the ground. I scrambled up, trying to figure out what was going on.

"Hello there, Tempest," my attacker said. One look at his pale, scarred skin and I recognized him instantly. It was the teleport from Chicago, the one Holocene and I had taken down. "My name is Sven."

"Hi, Sv—"

Sven slammed his fist into my face. My nose cracked and my head snapped back. Blood poured from my nose and a cacophony of ooh and aahs came from the people watching.

I tried to regain my composure, but another punch slammed into my stomach, sending my air flying from my lungs. I dropped to my knees, gasping for air.

Sven slammed his elbow into my back, throwing me to the floor. I was desperate to feel the popping sensation of my body healing itself, but all I felt was pain and the warmth of the blood pouring from my nose. I searched within me for my powers, trying to coax them out. All I found was static and pain.

Sven got on top of me and punched me in the face as hard as he could. I felt the bones in my face give a little and after a few more punches, they cracked. I screamed in pain, but could do nothing to fight back. Sven held me down and pummeled me, his face filled with calm rage. He had every intention of killing me.

Could he kill me? If my body couldn't heal itself, it was certainly possible. Surely the STF goons wouldn't allow that. They couldn't. Could they? I did make Director Loren *very* upset.

As if in answer to my question, the crackling of electricity sounded from Sven. His body went rigid and began convulsing as he fell in a seizing heap on the floor next to me.

I lay there moaning in pain. I could feel my face begin to swell. My vision began to blur and the black stars in my vision weren't going away.

I felt myself being lifted into the air, the sudden movement sending waves of pain crashing through me. The hands set me down on a gurney and my gaze fell on Hank.

He was sitting in the same position, drawing. I caught a glimpse of the image on his paper.

It was my own bloodied face.

The guards rushed me out of the room and once again all I could focus on was the immense pain.

Chapter 28
Doctors Orders

THE GUARDS WHEELED me into a room filled with bright lights. I looked around as best I could and saw the room was lined with people in suits, watching everything that was happening very closely.

"I need a smooth surface for the pods," I heard one doctor say to another.

A team of doctors was hovering around me, masks covering their faces. Some of them ripped my clothes off, leaving me bare and cold.

Every touch hurt. I was aware of everything. The pain that coursed through me, the static in my head, the doctors sliding a cool metal needle into my veins, the cold patches they placed on my chest.

The clippers shaving the hair from my head.

The vibrations sent such severe pain shooting through my head it was almost unbearable. I thought I was going to pass out. I could almost feel the bone fragments in my face shake around like rocks on a conveyer belt.

My hair fell in a pile around me, tickling my neck. Some clung to my eyelashes and I blinked it away. I couldn't even begin to imagine what they could be shaving my head for. I didn't even want to. All I wanted was to have my powers back. All I wanted was to have my regeneration back for just a split second. Just to heal myself a tiny bit—not even all the way. That's all. Was that too much to ask for? Had I not earned at least that?

"Okay, that's good," a doctor said. "Applying nodes."

I felt what felt like lots of small fingers digging into my head. It felt as if a masseuse was preparing to give me a thorough head massage. It would've felt good had I not been distracted by my broken face.

"Tempest, listen to me," a voice said. This was one I recognized. Loren.

I moved my eyes to meet hers. I could barely see through the slits they now were, thanks to the swelling.

"We're turning off your Eximus shocker for a few seconds. If you try anything, we'll bring Sven in here for another round. Understand?"

I tried to say something, but all that came out was a gurgling noise that she took for a yes.

"We're ready, ma'am," a doctor told her.

"Everybody stand back," she said, taking a step back herself.

I felt the static in my head fade away. The hum from the Eximus receded back into the device implanted into my neck.

And the popping began.

No, I told myself.

No! I screamed in my head.

I was trying to stop my regeneration.

I'd realized what they were doing. They were studying what was going on in my brain when I was healing myself.

I didn't know what they would learn from the readings they were gathering, but whatever it was, they sure as hell didn't need to know.

The popping didn't stop. I felt cracking around my eye socket as the bones fused back together.

"Stop it," I hissed under my breath.

A huge pop came from my jaw and I yelped in pain. "No! Stop it!" I spat.

"Don't fight it, Tempest!" Loren snapped. "There's no reason to fight it!"

"Screw you!" I yelled.

The bones in my body healed. I felt hair push out from my scalp, returning to the length it had been before they shaved it.

I was back at one hundred percent.

The static returned. My brain hummed. My powers were gone.

"We have the readings, ma'am. Mission successful," one of the doctors said.

"Thank you, Pollocks," Loren said. She walked into my line of sight, standing over me. "And thank you, Tempest." She flashed a condescending smile.

A doctor removed the device from my head. She ran her fingers through my hair. I tried to reach up to yank her hand away, but my hands were tied down. I hadn't even realized they'd restrained me.

"You did a good job. Keep it up."

CHAPTER 29
FAMILIAR VOICES

I WALKED INTO THE boys' dormitory of the building the STF was holding us in. There were a dozen twin-sized beds lined up and down each side of the room. At the back was a doorway that led to the locker room and showers, while up above was a similar glass window setup like the one in the living area.

I walked across the concrete floor, looking for a place to sleep. People watched me as I walked by, apparently puzzled by the fact that I was totally healed. I guessed they didn't let people use their powers often, like they had me. Then I realized that some of them might have not realized that I had regenerative powers, that maybe they'd thought I was just really tough or something. There were some powers there was no way they could know I had, like my super hearing or super vision. And if they didn't, the STF probably didn't either. Not that it helped me much in the situation I was currently in.

Most of the Supers in the room were in their own self-made groups. Not quite cliques, because they weren't so stereotypical. At least, not from what I could tell. It just seemed like two or three were in one corner, two or three more in another, etc., etc. I noticed Brian and Sven were in a group with two other people—a girl with black hair and olive skin and a dark-skinned man with a bald head and a serious case of Resting Bitch Face.

In the back of the room was a spot between Hank and another guy. I walked over there and stood in front of the empty bed. "Is this spot taken?" I asked.

Hank looked up at me from his notebook and smiled. "Good to see you survived. No, you can take it."

I nodded in thanks and sat down on the bed, then slipped off the white tennis shoes they'd provided me with. I looked over to the bed next to me and saw a Hispanic teen sitting there, writing on some paper. "Hey, my name's Tempest," I said to him.

He looked up at me, smiling. "Name's Wes."

"Nice to meet you, Wes." I gestured to his notebook. "Where do you get those?"

"They're in the Common Room," Hank said.

I turned to him. "Cool, I'll have to grab one." I craned my head to try to get a glimpse at what Hank was drawing, but I couldn't tell. I wanted to ask him about his drawing of me, but wasn't sure when I'd get the chance. It was definitely a conversation I wanted to have in private.

"That was a real scene Sven caused with you earlier," Wes said.

I turned my attention back to him. "Yeah, I guess. He seems like not a very nice guy."

"Especially since you're the one who beat him to a bloody pulp."

As if on cue, a man I recognized walked by. It was the guy from the bank in Dallas. He shot me a look as he passed, but didn't try anything. I got the message, though. I'd really have to watch my back.

My gaze turned to Brian, who was sitting on a bed, talking with his group. I figured his change of heart toward me wouldn't last. I was disappointed I was right, though. I'd been hoping he really had changed, but it seemed that his powers developing. The Eximus, or something, had changed him. He was now back to regular ol' Brian Turner and right now, I was regular ol' Kane Andrews.

Not Tempest.

Kane.

*

I lay in bed staring up. Ambient light filtered in through the viewing glass around the edges of the ceiling. The lights were off, and the rhythmic sounds of people breathing as they slept filled the room.

I took in a deep breath and winced. I still wasn't used to the overpowering smell of bleach and plastic.

"Jesus, that smell is awful," Samantha said in my head.

I nearly jumped out of my skin. On a computer screen somewhere, some technician probably saw my heart skip a few beats. "Holy shit, is that you, Samantha?" I whispered.

"The one and only."

Relief washed through me. I felt my body buzz, not from the Eximus energy. I felt as if my powers might return and I'd be able to fly out of this godforsaken place. "How long have you been in my head?"

"A while now. I was waiting to say something until I figured everyone was asleep."

I closed my eyes and breathed deep. I couldn't get over how good hearing her voice felt. "Thank you, Samantha," I whispered.

Her intoxicating chuckle echoed around my humming brain. "No problem. I couldn't give up on the other half of Samantha & Kane, LLC that easily."

"Oh, man, I bet our stocks have plummeted."

"It was a bloodbath on the trading floor," Samantha said, feigning sadness.

"Send our investors my condolences."

"Ha, speaking of which! One of our board members, a Ms. Holocene, is spending all of her time searching for you. We all are, Kane."

The thought of that touched me. Broke me. I found that my cheeks were suddenly wet. I reached up to touch them and realized I was crying. It was all too much. I had some amazing friends—family, really—who had my back. They wouldn't stop looking for me until I'd been found. I wasn't alone.

And I never would be.

"Samantha, thank you."

"Of course, Kane."

"So how are things going out there? Are my parents okay?" I asked, changing the subject.

"They're freaking out, of course, but I called them from a pay phone and explained what I could. Other than that, I'm starting to hear some troubling rumors about this Super. He calls himself Atlas. I don't even know what his powers are, but apparently he's gaining lots of followers every day. I don't know how or for what reason, but Doug and I are keeping an eye on the situation. We'll let you know what we find out."

"Okay, tha—"

Cold hands wrapped around my ankles and yanked me from my bed.

CHAPTER 30

BRAWL

MY HEAD SLAMMED into the ground and I saw stars. I became dizzy and disoriented, nausea washing over me. My body was being dragged across the cold cement floor.

"Kane, what's going on?" Samantha asked, growing frantic.

I didn't respond. I struggled against the person who had my ankles. I kicked and flailed, but it did nothing. I could see five figures, all rushing toward the locker room with me in tow.

I grabbed the legs of one of the empty beds as I passed, dragging it across the floor with me. It scraped across the floor, sending a loud screeching noise echoing around the room. People sat up in their beds, half-awake, trying to figure out what was going on.

Someone stomped on my hand, causing me to let go of the bed. I looked up and saw the one who'd done the stomping was Prime, the guy from the bank.

I flipped over onto my stomach, causing the person who was dragging me to cross their arms. They got tangled up and let go of me. I scrambled to my feet, but barely got running before someone wrapped their arms around me and threw me backwards.

I went flying through the doorway that separated the sleeping quarters from the locker room. I slid across the floor and slammed into the first row of lockers.

Brian, Sven and Prime entered the room, along with the black-haired girl and the dark-skinned guy.

Brian charged at me, his fist raised. I didn't get up at first. I waited until he begun to swing, then dove out of the way. Brian's fist slammed into the thin metal locker door, causing it to bend.

He howled in pain and I got up to my feet. I ran down the aisle of lockers to the showers in the back. My five pursuers were close behind.

The lights in the shower room were turned down very low, allowing for barely any light. The pipes seemed to zigzag on the wall and I ran to the nearest one. I grabbed it, yanking on it as hard as I could. I had more strength than usual, thanks to the adrenaline pumping through me, but it still wasn't enough.

The humming in my head subsided.

I hadn't been expecting that. I was in the middle of pulling on the metal bar and it came off the wall with ease. I stumbled backwards, trying my best not to fall.

The humming returned.

I looked up and saw Director Loren standing on the observation deck, watching with a sly smile.

I turned my attention to my five attackers, who had just entered the showers.

Once again, Brian lunged at me. I jumped to the side and brought my pipe down on his wrist. He fell to his knees, howling in pain. I slammed the pipe into the back of his head and he fell to the floor in a heap.

Pain exploded across my back. I'd turned my back to my attackers to take out Brian and they'd used that to their advantage.

I fell forward but turned around just in time to catch another punch to the face.

I swung my pipe around wildly. The edge of it scraped the girl attacker, causing a large gash on her face.

I felt a punch to my gut.

Another to my face.

The pipe was knocked from my hand.

Sven picked me up and slammed me to the floor. They started kicking me, hard. As hard as they could. I did my best to shield my ribs, but I knew it'd be impossible to prevent any of them from breaking.

But then the four sets of feet kicking me turned to three.

Someone had tackled Prime and was on top of him, punching his lights out.

Another slammed Sven into the wall behind me. I heard his nose crack, the sickening sound echoing around the shower tiles.

I grabbed the foot of the girl before her next kick landed. I twisted it and she fell to the floor.

More people flooded into the shower room and began attacking my attackers.

But then they started to fight back.

Sven punched Hank—the one who had slammed him into the wall—square in the throat. Hank grabbed his throat, unable to breathe.

I ran to Sven, grabbed his hair and slammed his head into

the shower wall. My anger took over and I slammed his head again. I pulled his head back, ready to slam it once more.

But someone tackled me off him. This person was someone I didn't recognize, but from the look on his face, he recognized me.

He punched me good in my stomach, but that was all he got in. I head-butted him, crushing his nose with my forehead. His hands clutched his bloody nose and he howled in pain. I grabbed his head and threw him off me into a heap on the floor.

Someone grabbed my shirt, but before they could throw me, I grabbed them. I threw them as hard as I could up against the wall and gave them a kick in the face. I went to kick them again, but they grabbed my foot and yanked on it. I almost slammed into the floor headfirst, but caught myself.

Cold water rained down on me. I looked up and saw that they'd turned on all the shower heads.

And that was when I saw what was really happening around me for the first time.

All the Supers were in the shower room, engaged in an all-out brawl. Blood mixed with water, swirling and snaking across the floor, searching for a drain to go down. There were probably around twenty people fighting each other in a dark shower room while cold water rained down on us.

The girl from earlier grabbed me and pulled me up. She was about to punch me, but before she could, I fell purposely to the floor. She hadn't been expecting that and because of the wet tiles, she fell to the floor with me. The only difference was that I was ready for the tumble.

We lay next to each other, drenched with cold water. I slammed my elbow into her stomach, and she exhaled in a big woof. I rolled over on top of her and wrapped my hands around her throat. Anger filled me. She was one of the ones who had started this all. She'd dragged me from my bed while I was talking to Samantha.

I hated her.

She gasped for air and grabbed at my wrists.

But then she decided to go a different route.

I was too close to her, so she clocked me on the side of my head. I fell to the floor, but recovered quickly. I was ready for more, but suddenly the Eximus shockers in our necks were turned up.

Everybody fell to the floor, writhing in pain. It amplified the pain I was already experiencing from the brawl. The electricity coursed through my head, but thankfully it stayed on the inside. It never came in contact with the water that covered the floor, thank god. That would not have ended well.

The pain began to recede and I felt two arms hook beneath mine. I was being pulled away by two STF guards. All the other Supers were still lying on the bloody, wet shower floors, incapacitated by the Eximus energy that flowed through them.

Chapter 31
Promises

I SAT RESTRAINED TO the same metal chair I'd been in when they brought me here. It felt as if I'd been sitting there for hours, but really it hadn't been that long at all.

I hurt all over. It didn't seem like they were going to let me heal, at least not yet. I looked around the room for any sign of people watching me, but there was no one. I was alone.

That is, until the door opened. Loren walked in and someone wheeled in a gurney behind her. The person left and it was just Loren, me and whatever what was on the gurney. It was covered up, but it had the shape of a body.

"That was quite the scene back there. I actually began to enjoy myself," Loren said. "I don't think he did, though." She pulled the sheet on the gurney back. Wes' dead body lay there, bloody and broken. "It seems he had his head bashed in. A shame. But he served his purpose."

I struggled against my restraints. I seethed in anger. I wanted nothing more than to see Loren lying on a gurney of her own. "You're sick, you know that?" I hissed.

"I am not!" Loren snapped. "I care about the protection of this country. Of this *world*. If some of your kind have to die, that's fine. In fact, that's great. That's the whole point of this. Your annihilation."

"Then why don't you just kill me, huh? Just do it already!" I screamed in her face.

"Trust me, you'll get what's coming to you. But not until we learn more from you, Tempest." Loren leaned in close. She put one of her hands next to my head and braced herself. "Like what your name is."

"Again with the name?" I said, rolling my eyes. "Why do you care?" I shouted in her face.

"BECAUSE YOU'RE A GHOST!" Loren screamed as loud as she could. Her face was full of rage and frustration. "We've gone through every bit of DNA we've gathered from you. All your pictures. EVERYTHING! NOTHING! There's *nothing* about you. WHO—*WHAT* ARE YOU?"

I laughed. "Careful, your crazy's showing."

Loren reached into her pocket and blasted my brain with Eximus energy. I convulsed in pain and screamed.

"WHO ARE YOU?" she screamed over my yells of pain. She turned the energy down and grabbed my shirt. She pulled me as close to her face as my restraints would allow. "I vow to you, I will find out who you are, Tempest. One way or the other, I will find out." She thrust a finger at Wes' lifeless body, lying on the gurney. "I let that happen. I could've stopped it, but I let it happen. People will die, Tempest. People you think are your allies will be your downfall. If you don't tell me who you are, I will kill everyone. Every last Super, until you tell me who you are. And if you don't? If I find out on my own? When I do, I will go after everyone you love. I will go after everyone you've ever talked to, looked at, or even thought about. I'll kill them all. Right in front of you. And after that's done, that's when I will kill you. The Supers will die with you and they will die by my hand. I promise you that. I promise you."

Director Loren let go of me and I fell back into my chair. She stormed out of the room, slamming the door behind her, leaving me there, alone with Wes.

CHAPTER 32
BRAINSTORMS

I LAY IN MY bed, Hank asleep next to me. I had no idea what time it was, but shortly after Loren had stormed out, some other people came in and set me free. They took me to get patched up and then brought me back to the bunkroom.

Every few minutes someone would stumble in, their arm in a cast, or with gauze wrapped around their head. They'd walk over to their bed and collapse.

It'd been a long night, but I wasn't able to find sleep.

"I wanna say something, but last time we were in this situation, things didn't go too well," Samantha said in my head.

I closed my eyes, comfort washing over me. "Yeah, that ordeal wasn't fun."

"From what I saw, I'd have to agree. I'm sorry, but I couldn't watch most of it. It was too much," she said, shame filling her voice.

"No, no, it's okay," I said, almost a little too loud. I brought my voice down. "I'm glad you didn't. I can only imagine what this all must be like for you. All of you guys, really."

"They'll be glad to hear that I'm in touch with you.

Hopefully we'll figure something out soon. But don't worry, we're going to get you out of there."

"I have faith that you will," I said. A few moments passed before I asked Samantha the question that had been bothering me. "Samantha, why do you think they want to know my name so bad?"

"Really? How about, why the hell they can't find anything about you in any government database?" she asked incredulously.

"Yeah, I'm trying not to even think about what that could mean."

"Who knows. I would say I'd get Doug to hack into a government database and see what we could find, but we'd need access to a government computer. Can't just go through the internet. We've done it once—that's how we were able to help you out with the whole nuke situation during the Richter crisis. But that's because they had satellite locations set up."

"Great minds," I said with a smirk, mostly to myself.

"What was that?"

"Nothing. But forget about the ghost thing for a minute. Why do they care so much about my name?"

"Maybe because they want what they can't have? I don't know. That seems kinda petty, doesn't it? Like they'd have bigger things to worry about."

"Exactly, which is what boggles my mind. Why isn't holding Tempest enough for them? They're the ones who gave the name to me in the first place."

"They might just want to know, maybe so they can learn more about the environment in which you developed your powers," Samantha said.

The door opened and a girl walked in holding an ice pack

to her head. I waited for her to walk to her bed and collapse on it before I responded to Samantha. "That could be it. Not trying to be cocky, but I'm probably the most powerful Super there is. I guess they *really* want to know how that happened."

"Exactly. Plus, since you killed Richter, you're the oldest—well, not oldest, but you've been a Super for the longest period of time. I don't blame them for wanting to know everything there is to know about you."

"Oh, you don't, do you?" I teased.

Samantha groaned. "You know what I mean, Kane. If they want to kill all the Supers, of course they want to know everything they can about the most powerful and oldest one."

"Yeah, I guess. It's probably a bit humiliating, too," I said. I thought about how angry and frustrated I was making Loren. It was nice having the upper hand, although her threats didn't sit well with me. Could she actually kill my family? And how many more people would die here inside the STF compound? On the other hand, how many more Supers would die if she found out my name? If she was able to figure out everything there was to know about me and thus, the Supers? It could lead to disaster.

I had a feeling everything was going to head that way, with or without my name.

CHAPTER 33
FRIENDLY FIGHTING

FOUR GUARDS STOOD at my sides, in front of and behind me as they led me down a long hallway. The walls were blank and the florescent bulbs cast a harsh light all around. I wasn't sure where they were leading me, but judging from the device on my head, it was to more experiments.

The device was the same one they had put on me whenever they allowed me to use my healing powers, so hopefully the fact that I had it on again meant that they were taking me somewhere where I would be granted my powers back. Hopefully I'd be able to use that to my advantage, which meant escaping.

They led me into a dark room where every surface was made of stainless steel—or at least something that looked like it. The guards turned and exited the room behind me, the door sealing shut with a hiss. I looked and there wasn't a single crack or seam where the door once was.

I felt a hum in the walls; it coursed through my fingers. It wasn't unlike the humming I felt in my brain.

The walls flashed with purple electricity as Eximus energy coursed through my body. I was sent flying back across the room, my body convulsing. A hissing sound came from across the room and a door identical to the one I had just come through opened up. Someone was pushed inside, then the doors sealed and the walls hummed with energy.

"This doesn't look good," the newcomer said. From the light of the Eximus energy in the walls and from his voice, I figured out it was Hank standing fifteen or twenty feet away from me. He was wearing the same type of device on his head that I was.

"Did they say anything to you?" I asked.

Hank shook his head. "They just brought me here. Said they'd give more insert—"

"Good evening, gentlemen," a voice said through a speaker in the ceiling, interrupting Hank. "You've been brought here for certain reasons. We'd like to see a good show, so please, don't go easy on each other."

The humming in my head subsided and strength flooded through me. I began to hover a few feet off the floor and couldn't believe how good it felt. It was like being stuck in a cramped car for hours and then finally being able to stretch your legs.

Something whipped past me and I realized I'd closed my eyes. I opened them to see Hank's arms stretched all the way across the room. Joy filled his face as he enjoyed the same 'stretching' sensation I was, except quite literally.

"*Whoo hoo!*" he hollered. His whole body began to stretch as he relished in the chance he had to use his powers.

"Gentlemen, I don't think you understand. *Fight.*"

The joy and euphoria left us instantly. Our eyes met, dread filling our faces.

"Do they really want us to fight?" Hank asked.

"Yes, we do," the person answered over the intercom before I could respond.

"I won't fight him!" I shouted. "I won't do it!"

"You don't have a choice in the matter, Tempest. Either you fight, or you tell us your name." This time I recognized the voice. It was that of Director Loren.

I flew as close to the ceiling as I could get without touching the Eximus that flowed through it. "You listen to me!" I shouted. "I will not fight! I will no—"

Hands wrapped around my chest and threw me to the ground. The floor cracked, exposing the subfloor that flowed with Eximus. Some of it zapped me and I jumped to the side, out of its way. I looked up and saw Hank standing there, his body retracting to its normal self.

"What are you doing?" I asked.

Hank didn't answer. He grabbed me and, using his arms like a slingshot, slammed me into the wall. I was thrown backwards by the power of the Eximus and into the floor.

"We have to fight!" Hank yelled. "It's the only way!"

"Hank, I'll kill you. I can't fight you," I said as I stood.

Hank stretched his arm back as far as he could and then rocketed it forward. It slammed into my jaw, sending me backwards once again. "You underestimate me, Tempest."

He was really beginning to piss me off.

I stood up again and after deciding there was no other choice, dashed to his side and kicked his feet out from beneath him. Hank fell to the floor with a thud, but reached out and grabbed one of my ankles.

I tripped and slammed to the floor. I rolled head over heels, leaving a destroyed floor in my wake. I got up slowly and turned to face Hank. He was standing at the other side of the room, the floor between us ripped up from my tumble.

We waited. We looked up at the ceiling, looking for any sign from the people who were watching us.

"You're not finished," a voice said.

I opened my mouth to yell something at them, but was thrown back by the momentum of Hank wrapping himself around me over and over again, squeezing as tight as he could. I felt my bones begin to bend beneath the pressure he was exerting on me. I could barely move as he wrapped himself around my face, causing my world to go black. I gasped for air, but there was none. I tried to move, but was completely immobile. Bones began to snap and crack as he squeezed tighter. I was completely helpless.

Even though all I could see was black, I still saw flashes as stars began to paint my vision. My lungs screamed out for air, but they were paralyzed.

I couldn't fight back. In my head, I began to wave a white flag. I was stunned.

That's enough, I heard someone say in the distance. The voice was faint and fading.

Hank began to unwrap himself and I felt my body rush to repair itself. I gasped for air once I was free, filling my power return to me.

Then I felt the humming in my head again. The Eximus inside me was switched back on and I was back to being Kane Andrews, not Tempest. And neither one of us could believe we had just been beaten by Hank.

CHAPTER 34
PSEUDONYMS

I SAT ALONE AT a table in the common room. I stared at my lunch of a ham and cheese sandwich and crackers and felt no appetite. All I could think about was the fight with Hank, how he had been able to gain the upper hand. I liked to think that given a little bit more time, I would've figured out a solution, but I couldn't be sure. Still, I couldn't help but fight the feeling that I was lying to myself. That if Hank had kept going, I would've passed out, my body slipping me into a coma until I got more oxygen.

"Hey, there, how's lunch today?" Samantha asked, popping into my head.

"I'll let you know if I get around to eating it," I said under my breath, looking around to make sure no one was around to hear my one-way conversation.

"Not hungry today?" she asked, concerned.

I shrugged. "Just not feeling it. How are things out there?"

She hesitated, then said, "They're getting...tense. More and more Supers are making their presence known every day. Holocene is doing what she can to stop the bad ones—which is 99.9% of them—but she's just one person and she's distracted by her search for you."

"Tell her not to worry about me. I can figure something out on my own," I said.

"No way," Samantha snapped. "We're not giving up on you, not even close. Holocene is putting a lot of attention on finding you, because she knows once she does, keeping the Supers under control will be a lot easier. We need you, Kane."

I wanted to slam my fist down on the table, but stopped myself so as to not attract attention. I felt so helpless. They didn't need Kane, they needed Tempest. And he was hiding somewhere in my brain, kept at bay by the Eximus energy constantly flowing through me. "I'm sorry, Samantha," was all I could end up saying.

"It's okay, Kane. It's not your fault. *I'm* sorry it's taking so long to find you. These guys are very secretive."

I changed the subject. "What's the word on this Atlas guy you were talking about the other night? He still around?"

"Yes and no." I didn't like the sound of that. Samantha continued, "I've heard whispers—Doug too—about more and more Supers joining his cause. It doesn't even seem like the Super Task Force is fully aware of them yet, or they aren't taking them as a threat."

"I've got their hands a little full, I think." I smirked. "But are they a threat?"

"I don't know. They don't seem to have lots of powerful Supers, but their numbers are growing. They're calling themselves the Legion of Richter."

My heart froze. "So you mean they're basically an army of Richters?"

"Well, none of them seem as powerful as he was, but it

seems they're taking up his mantle. His ideals." Fear crept into Samantha's voice.

"Tell me what you can about this Atlas guy. I need to know for when I get out of here."

"Tempest," a voice behind me said.

Four guards were standing there, Eximus guns at the ready. "I'm eating lunch," I said.

"Doesn't matter. You're needed for more testing."

"I just did testing this morning," I said, my frustration growing.

"You think one test on one morning gets you a 'get out of testing free' card? Get your ass up, or else we'll turn a blind eye and let some of these Supers get their hands on you like they've been itching to," the guard threatened.

"Go, Kane. Don't get yourself killed. We need you out here, remember?" Samantha said.

I stood and followed the guards out the door, but only because of Samantha's urging.

I was led into a white room with a wall of thick glass down the middle. The walls were plain and bare—no Eximus energy in sight. It seemed I wasn't going to be getting my powers back for this test, which disappointed me. I longed to feel my feet floating off the floor, or the way the world slowed when I ran as fast as I could.

"Instructions will follow," the guard said. He and his goons exited the room, the lock on the door engaging as he shut it behind him.

Once again, the scientists were up in the viewing chambers, preparing for whatever test would be next.

The door on the other side opened to admit a guy about my age named Rai. From the little bit of talking with him that I'd done, I considered him one of the good guys.

Behind him stood Sven. From the little hand-to-hand fighting I'd done with him, I considered him one of the bad guys.

A queasy feeling grew in my stomach. I had a bad feeling about what would happen next.

"Hello, Tempest. My name is Loren. What's yours?" Director Loren asked in a patronizing tone from the observation deck up above.

"Oh, just Loren, is it? No last name? Guess I'm not the only one who likes to keep their name a secret," I said.

"Sven, you've been briefed. Do what you wish," Loren said.

My attention shot to where Sven and Rai were standing. I began to run through the possibilities of what could happen.

And then Sven's fist smashed into Rai's face.

Rai fell to the ground, blood spurting from his nose. Sven slammed his fist into Rai as he tried to get up.

The lump in the pit in my stomach grew. I wanted to scream as loud as I could. I wanted to get Sven to stop. I wanted to smash through the glass and do to Sven what he was doing to Rai.

But I couldn't.

All I could do was cry.

Not sob, but tears did drip from my eyes.

I cried because there was nothing I could do. I was helpless and so was Rai.

Sven grabbed him and slammed his head against the floor. Rai cried out in pain and tried to defend himself. But Sven was large and muscular, while Rai was skin and bones. Maybe he had some sort of power that allowed him to grow huge muscles and be superstrong at the snap of a finger, but at that moment, he had nothing. His only hope was me.

Sven began to kick him. I could've sworn I heard ribs crack. Even if I didn't hear it for real, though, I knew it was happening. As hard as Sven was kicking him, how could it not?

"Please stop," I whispered. It was all I could do. If I gave up my name, Loren would win. The STF would know everything about Kane Andrews to go along with all they knew about Tempest. They'd be able to learn the conditions under which my powers had developed. They'd be able to go after my friends, my family. There was no telling what all they could learn about the Supers, maybe even what it would take to destroy all of us and keep us from ever coming back. "Please, stop!" I yelled louder.

I rushed to the glass. I found my voice. I slammed my fists against the glass, just like Sven was slamming his into the bloody mess that was Rai.

"Stop this, please! You have to stop! He's not a Super! Right now he's human! You can't do this!" I yelled, my hands beginning to hurt from hitting the glass over and over and over.

"You know what you have to do, Tempest. You know." The satisfaction in Loren's voice was sickening.

Desperate to do whatever it took to make Sven stop, I yelled out a lie. "Derek Porter! My name is Derek Porter!"

Sven fell to the ground, the Eximus shocker in his neck giving him a extra dosage.

"It's nice to meet you, Derek. My name is Loren Westlake."

I fell to the ground, out of breath, emotionally spent. It was anything but a happy introduction, because once they found out I wasn't Derek Porter, I doubted the result would be pretty. But there had to be a lot of Derek Porters. Sorting through all of them would probably take a while. I'd bought myself some time and Rai was no longer being beat to a pulp. That was what mattered, even if I had a feeling it would come back to bite me.

Please hurry, Holocene, I thought. *Please.*

Chapter 35

Enter the Dome

"SO ATLAS AND his group are just leaving giant Rs everywhere? That's it?" I asked Samantha.

I was sitting in the same chair I'd been sitting in before the whole Rai/Sven situation went down. Except now it was dinner I was picking at, still not hungry at all.

"Yeah, in all the major cities. Nothing else, though. They aren't destroying anything, killing anybody, nothing. Super activity has been down today too. I don't know if that means anything, but if it keeps up, it can't mean anything good."

"Well, the lack of bad Supers going crazy is never that bad of a thing," I said.

"To some extent. If it's been down because all the Supers are joining Atlas and the Legion of Richter, that can't be good," Samantha said.

"But you don't know that's what's happening."

"It's what I've been hearing. It makes sense, too. If he has a plan, he wouldn't want his people out there going crazy and wreaking havoc."

I sighed. I wanted to be out there investigating this with

Samantha and the rest of the crew so bad. "Can't you get into Atlas' head? See what he's up to?"

Samantha groaned. "You have no idea how many times I've been asked that question. I can only get into the heads of people I know a lot about. I have to be able to picture them in my head, or believe they're sitting across the table from me."

"You got into mine and you didn't know anything really concrete about me," I pointed out.

"You were all over the news. I couldn't get away from you. I saw what you looked like as Tempest and was able to put together enough pieces. It was still *really* hard, though. It took me forever. Atlas? No one is really talking about him. The media doesn't know he exists, neither does the general public, and I don't even know if the STF does. I can't picture him in my head. Knowing what a person looks like is more than half the battle."

I sighed and fought the urge to lay my head down on the table. I was so tired. Tired of everything, and nothing in particular. This whole ordeal was wearing on me in ways I couldn't quantify.

Luckily for me, it was all close to being over.

I walked with the rest of the Supers in a single file line. There were about thirty of us in total, all of us wearing the headgear I wore every time I used my powers. The fact that all of us were wearing one and were marching off somewhere unsettled me greatly. There was no telling what we were marching off to.

Up ahead, situated in the wall, was an automatic door. As we got closer, the door had slid to the side, inviting us outdoors. We were being marched into a giant domed arena.

It felt like we were about to play football or something. Like all of us were a team headed down the tunnel, about to walk into an arena filled with cheering fans.

"Everybody stop here!" the guard at the front said.

Everybody halted, including all the guards who had come out there with us.

"Make a single file line in this direction!" he shouted, gesturing left-to-right. Everybody began lining up and I found myself standing next to Hank.

"Any idea what's going on?" I asked under my breath.

Hank shrugged. "Maybe it's Thanksgiving and we're about to have the annual football game."

"If it's shirts versus skins, I call shirts," I said.

"What kind of family did you grow up with that played shirts versus skins on Thanksgiving?" Hank asked, looking me up and down with a curious look on his face.

"We're going to play a bit of a game," the head guard said. "Practice, if you will. You will go inside the Eximus dome and be given your powers back. You will try to defeat our STF soldiers, who will be hunting you down."

Right on cue, the Super Task Force soldiers came around a corner and began marching over toward us. They marched in unison, not a single one of them carrying a gun at his side. They lined up in formation, creating a funnel that led to the entrance of the dome.

"Enter the dome," the guard said, and we began marching in.

Fire rose inside of me, along with hope. I was going to get my powers back. Even though I would be surrounded by the Eximus, I had a fighting chance to escape.

I looked into the eyes of the soldiers as we walked by. They looked more intense than the regular guards, and they were wearing armor that buzzed with Eximus energy. They were standing at the ready, looking straight ahead.

Except for one. One of the guards was looking right at me. I looked directly back at him, then I realized why he was watching me.

I knew him.

It was Drew. He worked for the STF, and he was about to practice hunting me down.

CHAPTER 36
THE FIRST BATTLE

I WALKED INTO THE Eximus Dome in total shock—pun not intended. Standing out there, about to hunt me and the other Supers, was my best friend Drew. How could he do something like this?

Then it started to click. He'd told me he had powers. He'd told me he'd been gone for a few months too. He'd been dropping hints, and I never caught on. I suddenly got the feeling that—like me—he hadn't been volunteering to help rebuild during those lost months.

"You have five minutes to make preparations," a voice said over the loudspeaker.

Fights between the Supers broke out immediately. Rai used his shape shifting powers to turn his arm into a sharp object and thrust it through Sven. I guess he didn't know that Sven had regenerative powers, because the look of surprise on his face when he pulled his arm out and Sven was still standing was genuine.

A blast of heat hit my back and I jumped out of the way. I turned and saw Brian had begun to attack me, shooting flames from his hand. I saw a building nearby and jumped six stories on top of it. I looked around the dome, looking for any way to escape. Inside the dome was a fake city, complete with cars, street vendors, and city blocks. Behind me a small portion of the area was set up to be like a forest, while another looked to be an open desert. In all, the dome was the size of two football fields in both length and width.

I looked down at the brawl taking place below, where Hank was fighting with the girl who had attacked me in the showers a few nights ago, Beatrice. With a name like that, I could understand why she seemed so angry all the time. She had laser vision, but was having a hard time hitting Hank. He kept dodging out of the way just in time and getting a couple more hits on her.

But then I saw a huge guy named Barry charging at him, and Hank had no idea. Barry had super strength, and if he blindsided Hank, it wouldn't end well.

I jumped off the building head first, my hands to my sides. I flew toward the ground like a bullet, but swooped up just in time. I flew over the heads of the fighting Supers, sending those who weren't on steady footing stumbling backward. I flew past Barry and grabbed Hank, pulling him up in the air.

Beatrice jumped out of the way just in time to not get run over by Barry.

I flew to the building I'd been standing on earlier and set Hank down. "You good?" I asked.

"Y-yeah...I'm good," Hank said, out of breath.

"Kane, what's going on? Are you out?" Samantha asked frantically.

"No, some sort of exercise. Samantha, did you know anything about Drew working for the STF?" I asked.

"Who are you talking to?" Hank asked, but I ignored him.

"Oh my god, I had no idea! You mean he's known where they've been keeping you this entire time?"

"I think so. I'm about to find out exactly where that's at once I find him. Make sure Holocene's ready. I'm getting out of here *today.*"

"Good, because I need to tell you something. The Legion of Richter is mobilizing. Atlas and his strongest soldiers are going somewhere to do something, but we don't know what yet. It can't be good, though."

It looked like I wouldn't be getting any R&R once I got out. "Okay, I'll be out of here soon. Don't worry, everything's going to be okay," I said. I believed it, too. Just knowing that I'd be out soon made me feel invincible. Even though I pretty much was out already, I felt confident. The cards were turning out to be in my favor.

"Five minutes is up," a voice said over the loudspeakers.

I turned to Hank. "You stay here, I'll be back. We're getting out of here today, Hank."

Hank looked at me with wide eyes and nodded, like I was crazy.

"Don't worry," I said with a smirk. "The voice in my head is a real person, and she's going to help get us out of here."

I turned away, toward the entrance. The doors that led to the holding bay opened and out walked STF Soldiers.

Then I realized why they didn't have guns: because all of them were Supers. Every single one of them had purple Eximus electricity jumping and crackling from their arms. I scanned the faces as they marched to the playing field, searching for Drew.

I found him. Third row, far right.

It was time to get some answers.

I flew down and grabbed Drew by the back of his armor, being careful not to touch his skin. I realized that the Eximus energy wasn't coming from him, though; his powers were off. I flew toward the forest and landed near the back wall of the dome.

Drew looked around frantically. It happened so fast, he hadn't even realized what was going on.

"You have some explaining to do," I said, not dialing back the anger in my voice.

"That's rich, coming from you," Drew said, taking a step toward me. "I'll explain everything later, but right now we need to get out of here."

"And why should I trust you?" I said.

In a quick swooping motion, Drew activated his powers, slid behind me, and smashed his finger into the back of my neck. I felt an intense heat and a surge of pain. I jumped forward, ready to fight Drew even though that was the last thing I wanted.

"I just overloaded your Eximus generator. It's been destroyed, so they can't remotely take away your powers," Drew explained. "Take your headgear off."

I pulled the device off my head, threw it to the ground and smashed it with my foot.

"Do you trust me now?" Drew asked.

"A bit more than I did five minutes ago. Tell me where we are," I said.

"I don't know the exact location. They brought us here in a blacked-out bus. I do know that it's somewhere in the Oregon woods, near the coast. Should be easy to spot from the sky."

"You get that, Samantha?" I asked.

"Yep, telling Holocene now," she responded.

"Who was that?" Drew asked.

"Backup. What's next?" I asked.

"I'm going to overload this section of the force field like I did your generator. I'll only be able to take out this small section, though. Go grab your friends and bring them back here. Once we're out of here, I'll explain everything," Drew said, then walked towards the force field wall.

I hesitated for a second, taking a long look at Drew. He seemed genuine, and he *had* destroyed the tracker in my neck. Even if this was all just a ruse and he was trying to trick me, I had my powers back and they weren't going anywhere. I'd have to stay on my toes, but I felt as if I could take care of any situation that might arise.

I flew toward where the battle was taking place. When I reached the building where I had left Hank I saw that Sven had teleported himself up there. Sven knocked Hank to the ground just as I got close. I sped up and turned in the air, slammed into Sven feet first, and sent him flying off the building.

"Thanks for that," Hank said as I helped him up.

"Looked like you could use some help. Come on, we're getting out of here," I told him. Then I grabbed him and flew him back to Drew.

Drew had both of his hands on the force field, the Eximus flowing through him. He grunted and groaned, concentrating as hard as he could on overloading the force field.

I turned and flew back toward the fight, searching for Rai. He was fighting one of the STF Soldiers, dodging the punches from their Eximus-infused skin.

I swooped down and grabbed him, then flew back to Drew and Hank.

Once I'd set Rai down, Drew let out a shout. I could taste the electricity in the air as a twenty-foot section of the wall sparked. The purple Eximus energy stopped flowing on that section. There were burn marks all over and it looked as if it was in bad shape.

I walked up to it and touched it, jerking my hand away quickly just in case. Nothing. I touched it again, holding my hand on it for a bit longer. It had worked. Drew had shut it down.

I turned and looked back at Drew, Rai, and Hank, smiling, then punched the wall as hard as I could. That section of the wall exploded outward, and I took a step outside.

We were free.

Chapter 37
Escape

DREW DESTROYED THE generators on Hank and Rai. "We need to get out of here fast. The guards will be on their way any time now," he said once he was done.

"Okay, give it a few seconds. Holocene should be here any moment," I said.

I looked up to the sky and saw a blur fly by, another right behind it. The blur came back and hovered over the complex. It was Holocene. Next to her was a dark-skinned guy who was carrying a blonde girl on his shoulders. "Down here!" I shouted, waving my arms.

Holocene and the guy flew down, landing in front of us. Holocene walked toward me and wrapped her arms around me. I hugged her back. It was an incredible feeling, knowing I was actually going to escape. With Holocene and her new friends here, I felt as if we could take on anything.

"I'm so glad you're safe," Holocene said, pulling away. "I'm so sorry it took us so long."

"Don't worry about it. We're going to have to save introductions for later," I said, nodding toward the people she'd brought with her.

"Right. Let's get you all out of here," she said, looking at the guys standing behind me.

Something else caught my eye. All the purple Eximus energy that had been flowing through the dome had stopped. It had turned into a regular metal dome.

A blur fell from the sky and crashed into the roof of the dome. I could hear it slam into the ground inside.

"What the hell was that?" Drew said.

"Oh, no," Holocene said. She turned and looked up at the sky and the rest of us followed her gaze.

A group of ten Supers flew in, each of them carrying another on their back, except for the one flying at the front. Some of them flew through the hole their friend had made, while three of them landed around Holocene and the rest of us.

They were all wearing long black jackets and had what looked like body armor on underneath their shirts, but I couldn't tell for sure.

The one in the middle stepped forward, tall and confident. His black hair was slicked back, perfectly shaped. He looked at me with evil, menacing eyes. They were colored purple, a shade I'd never seen in person before. He walked with power, like he knew he could take each and every one of us down in a second. "How nice to meet you, Tempest," he said in a calm voice, looking right at me. His tone was patronizing, his smile not genuine.

"What makes you think I'm Tempest?" I said. He had no way of knowing. I wasn't wearing my costume and this was the first time we'd seen each other—in costume or not.

"I know a lot of things. If you'll just give my men and me a moment, we'll be taking care of this STF scum. Don't go anywhere, though. We have a lot to discuss," he said with a smile. He hovered in the air for a moment, as did his henchmen, then they flew into the dome.

I watched them disappear in disbelief. I wasn't going to stick around to ask questions. "Let's get out of here fast, guys," I said.

I grabbed Drew and put Rai on my back, while Holocene took Hank. The girl she'd brought climbed onto her other friend's back.

One of the buildings in the complex exploded to my right. I jumped into the air and we all flew out of there as fast as we could.

It was time to figure out exactly what was going on.

Chapter 38
The Name of the Enemy

DIRECTOR LOREN LOOKED at the wreckage of her STF Complex from her helicopter. It had been a little over eight hours since the Legion of Richter had attacked, and she was just as angry as she'd been when she found out. She had been in Washington D.C., trying to secure more funding for her project. As soon as she found out about the attack, she'd flown back to Oregon as fast as she could.

Looking upon the wreckage of what she'd worked so hard to build, she felt her anger grow.

"Land over there," she said to the pilot, pointing to a clear spot outside her Eximus Dome.

The helicopter landed and she stepped out, three guards following her. She looked at the sight. All the Supers had escaped and their generators and trackers had been destroyed. She was back at square one. Her complex had been destroyed, her people killed; everything was gone. Even Agent York was dead, the poor bastard. Nobody stood a chance, not even the Eximus soldiers she was so proud of. They were all gone.

She walked through one of the holes in the front of the dome. The fake city on the inside was rubble. Nothing was left standing. She kept walking toward the wreckage, stepping past the bodies of her soldiers as she did so.

She stepped onto the city street and took everything in. She still couldn't believe that all her hard work was gone. Not only that, but she'd never figured out Tempest's name. Secretly, that frustrated her more than anything. There was so much to learn from him. So much that could've stopped this from happening. But he had to be stubborn. He'd refused to tell her his name, and now she had no idea where he was. She had no way to make him pay.

"Who's there?" a female voice said from behind some rubble.

Loren almost jumped out of her skin. She rushed over to where the voice had come from, her guards following close behind. Behind a wrecked car covered in concrete and a street pole sat one of her Eximus soldiers, a young girl with black hair. She was dirty and her clothes had rips and tears in them. She was scraped up and in bad shape, but alive. Her hand were resting on the chest of someone, a small amount of Eximus energy coming from it.

Loren fell to her knees next to the girl and began checking to be sure she was all right. She felt a motherly duty set in. The Eximus soldiers were her pride and joy, and she'd thought they were all gone. She would do whatever it took to keep this one alive. "Are you okay?"

"I think so. I've been hiding here for a while with this Super," the girl said, gesturing with her head to her captive.

Loren recognized him. He was the one who controlled fire. "Wake him up," she said.

The soldier nodded and gave the Super a jolt of electricity.

He sat up, gasping for air. The Eximus soldier kept a hand on him, making sure he didn't get his powers back.

"Hello, there," Loren said. "What's your name again?"

"B-B-Brian T-Turner," he said through gritted teeth. She could tell he was in a lot of pain. "Please let me g-go."

Loren's face grew dark and she furrowed her brows. "I'm the one asking the questions here, Brian."

"I know something. I know something y-you want to know. If I tell you, will you let me go?"

Loren's interest was piqued. She figured *what the hell.* It wasn't like she had to keep her word. "Sure, Brian. What do you know?"

"I know who Tempest is. He went to school with me. I can tell you his name."

Loren's eyes flared and her breath caught. She couldn't believe it. If Brian was telling the truth, she was about to find out who Tempest was. She wouldn't be at square one anymore. She had an ace up her sleeve and she hadn't even known it until now. "Tell me."

"Kane Andrews. Tempest is a guy named Kane Andrews," Brian said.

Loren smiled. It was the first time in a long time that she'd actually, genuinely smiled. She was back on top. She had what she needed. She'd just been given the key to figuring the Supers out. Now, she wouldn't stop until she knew everything about Kane Andrews, all the way down to what he'd had for breakfast every day of his life. If there was a secret to destroying the Supers for good, that secret lay with Kane Andrews. And she was going to find it.

"Thank for that information, Brian," Loren said. She stood and retrieved her gun from its holster. "You're released."

"No wa—" Brian called out, but he was cut off by a gunshot.

Loren had put a bullet between his eyes.

She put her gun away and reached down to help the Eximus soldier up. Her very last one. "Why are you smiling?" Loren asked when she saw the look on the girl's face.

"I just think it's funny that Tempest's name is Kane Andrews."

"Why's that?" Loren asked.

"Because my name is Cassidy Andrews. Crazy coincidence, huh?"

Loren looked the girl up and down. "Yes, a crazy coincidence."

Part III:
The Siege of the Supers

Chapter 39

Waking Up

LEOPOLD RENNER BLINKED his eyes open, the whole room around him appearing blurry. He lifted his hands up to rub them into focus. When he did so, he felt wires and tubes that were attached to him rise up as well.

Once he could see better, he looked down and saw that he was hooked up to all sorts of machines that monitored his vitals and gave him an IV, as well as other medical things.

"It's good to see you, Leo," someone said to his right.

Leo turned his head and saw Kane Andrews standing there, smiling at him.

"W-where…" Leo tried to speak, but his mouth was too dry.

"Here, drink this," someone to his left said. He turned and saw the brunette girl who had been in the car with him earlier standing there. She pressed a cup into his hand.

Leopold grabbed the cup and drank the water from it. He felt the nasty, dry taste peel from his mouth. Now that he felt refreshed, her name popped into his head. "You're Selena. Holocene."

Selena nodded. "That's right."

"It's good to see you remembered," Kane said.

Leo turned his head to his right. "What's going on? Where am I?"

"First, I need to show you something." Kane was holding something behind his back. He revealed a mirror, facing away from Leo. "Take a good look into this mirror."

Kane flipped the mirror around and Leo saw himself staring back. But it wasn't quite himself. It wasn't the Leopold Renner who was in his mid-thirties; he looked the same as he had when he was twenty years old. But that couldn't be right. Not at all.

A beeping noise intensified as Leo's heart rate increased. "How is this possible?" An explanation landed in his head. "Is this some sort of time travel?"

Kane and Selena laughed. Kane shook his head. "No, of course not. I will explain everything."

Leo looked back into the mirror. He couldn't believe what he was seeing.

The whole building shook and an explosion sounded in the distance.

"What the hell was that?" Leo asked, looking around for some sort of explanation.

"That, Leo, is the war. It's what we're going to end—together," Kane said with a smile.

A door to the room opened and a girl with blonde hair rolled in in a wheelchair. "We've got some Legion ships incoming. We need the both of you up top ASAP," she said.

Selena and Kane met eyes and nodded.

"Thanks, Samantha. We're on our way," Kane said.

The girl Leo assumed was Samantha rolled out of the room in her wheelchair, closing the door behind her.

"You try to rest, okay? When you get your strength back, then we'll talk," Kane said, placing a hand on Leo's shoulder.

Leopold nodded, his head still spinning from all the questions he had without answers. Kane and Selena left the room, leaving Leo lying there all alone, listening to the sounds of the war raging on in the distance.

Chapter 40
Detour

I LANDED ON TOP of a building as we crossed into California.

"What are you doing?" Samantha asked.

"I gotta do something really quick," I told her. I set down Hank and Drew.

Drew looked at me and sighed, knowing what was next.

"You need to start talking, and fast," I said.

Drew crossed his arms. "Look, I understand why you didn't tell me you were Tempest. Trust me, I've seen the things that the STF can do, and I know you were just trying to keep me safe. Still, it kinda sucks."

"I'm sorry I didn't say anything, but like you said, I was just trying to keep you and everybody else safe. How did you get mixed up with the STF?"

"Well, I wasn't entirely lying when I said I'd been volunteering with the relief and rebuilding efforts. Late one night, I was wandering around one of the sites we were working on, just getting some fresh air. I ran across some STF people gathering samples for research. I started freaking out, saying I was going to call the cops, not realizing that they were government people. They captured me and I was put into a tiny cell without any windows. They left me there for a while before they finally came to me and told me that I could either join them or spend the rest of my life in prison. Of course I joined. The main reason they were interested in me was because I was from Ebon, and they knew Tempest—you—were from somewhere around there. So they trained me, implanted devices in me that give me my abilities, and sent me back to Ebon to keep an eye out for any Super activity."

"So your powers aren't naturally developing?" I asked.

Drew shook his head. "No, they're not. I don't know how they did it, but they allow me to control the Eximus energy. Not everyone can do it. Some people had terrible reactions to the devices and died."

The idea of the STF experimenting on humans without Super abilities disgusted me. I couldn't believe the government was allowing something like this to happen. "What made you turn against them?"

"Well, I was never really with them. I just didn't want to spend the rest of my life in prison. The pay wasn't bad, either. But when I knew for sure you were Tempest, I had to get you out of there. They'd end up killing you, and I couldn't let that happen. I tried to warn you before they captured you, but I wasn't one hundred percent sure it was you. I had my suspicions, and after a while I was able to put the pieces together. That's why I told you about my powers, so maybe you would shed some light on it on your own. I had to be sure it was you before I just started telling you all these things. But then they trapped you with that whole Delvin mission thing, and it was too late."

I stood there for a moment, thinking about what Drew

had just told me. It all sounded true, and if it was, it wasn't like Drew had much of a choice. I would've joined the STF too if my only other option was prison. I looked to Hank, who was standing off to the side trying not to get in the way. I knew he was listening, and he didn't seem to be disturbed or upset about anything Drew had said. I guess he believed him too.

"Okay," I said, coming to a decision. "I believe you."

I've never seen someone so relieved. Drew smiled and shifted his weight around on his feet. "Yeah, okay. Thanks, man. I'm really sorry."

"No, I'm sorry. Thankful, too. I don't know how I would've gotten out without you." I smirked. "Definitely would've found a way, though."

Drew chuckled. "I don't doubt it."

"You guys ready to go meet up with Samantha and the rest of the group?" I asked.

"Yes, they are. Get your ass over here," Samantha practically yelled in my mind. She was growing very impatient.

"Yeah," Drew said. "Let's go."

Chapter 41
Hello World

MY ALARM SOUNDED, waking me from a deep sleep. It'd been two days since I had returned home, and it felt as if I'd slept the entire time. Even if I wasn't that tired, there was just something about lying in my own bed that automatically put me to sleep.

I got up and began getting ready for the day. It was a Monday, so I had to go to school. Not to go to class, but to clean out my locker. My parents and I had decided that the safest thing for me to do would be to finish up my senior year from home. I wasn't sure how I felt about being homeschooled, but I didn't have much school left to do. By that logic I probably could've just stayed in high school, but with Atlas and the Legion of Richter out there planning whatever they were planning, I had no idea when I'd be called into action. Homeschooling was really my only option if I didn't want people to find out who I really was.

I wouldn't be doing it alone, though. Drew and his family were moving to Indianapolis, and the two of us would do school together. Drew's parents knew he'd been working with the STF. They'd been threatened to keep quiet even more than Drew himself had been. They were glad he wasn't working with them any longer; however, unlike me and my family, the STF knew exactly who Drew was. They'd have to use false names and lie low unless they wanted the STF to find them.

Not that there was much of an STF left, anyway. Atlas and the Legion had done a number on the complex. Holocene and I did a couple of flybys, and we saw that the entire place had been destroyed. It looked like everyone was dead, too. Hopefully the STF believed Drew was one of the casualties.

I brushed my teeth and stared blankly at my reflection in the mirror. Everything felt weird to me. Surreal, like I was in the middle of a transitioning period. So many things were happening that the general population didn't know about, but were bursting at the seams to find out. It wouldn't be long until Atlas and the Legion made their presence known, and I was sure the STF wouldn't be far behind. Which meant my team and I would have to be there to stop both of them from causing everything to fall apart.

Whether or not we'd be able to do that, I wasn't sure.

But those were Tempest's troubles. Right now, I was just Kane Andrews, and Kane Andrews had to go face Ebon High School one last time.

*

I dumped a bunch of papers into a trash bin I'd dragged over from nearby. I put the belongings I didn't want thrown away into my backpack, doing so as fast as I could. I wanted to get out of there before someone I knew ran into me.

Of course, someone did, and it was the last person I wanted to see.

"Hey, Kane," she said from behind me.

I turned in the empty hallway and saw Macy standing there, holding her books in front of her. Her sad smile caused my heart to flutter. Nostalgia flooded me and I couldn't help but think about how much I loved hanging out and talking with her. How much I missed it.

"Hey, Macy. Shouldn't you be in class?" I said, looking down the hallway toward the closed classroom doors.

"Yeah, I guess. I was just coming back from the restrooms and saw you. Are you leaving?" she asked, gesturing toward my half-empty locker.

"Yeah." I shrugged. "There's just too much here, you know? Too many bad memories." I mentally kicked myself. Why was I making myself seem like the victim?

"I get that. You've missed a lot of days lately."

"Yep," I said. I went back to cleaning out my locker. I just wanted her to leave, not because I didn't want to talk to her, but because I didn't like the feelings I got when I did. I didn't even know why she was being so nice to me.

"I just wanted to say that I'm sorry," she said, putting a hand on my shoulder.

I flinched and turned around. "It's okay, Macy. Don't worry about it. I was being selfish by not explaining anything to you. I just have a lot going on right now, and I need some space."

She nodded as she shifted back and forth on her feet. "Of course, I get that. I just hate that everybody's leaving," she said. I noticed her eyes were beginning to water. "I mean, you, Drew, and Michael were the reasons I wanted to stay. Now everybody's gone. Even Brian. I haven't talked to him in weeks and I'm just so scared, Kane. I'm so afraid. I don't know what's going on with anybody and I'm just an outsider. I should've gone back to Indianapolis. I shouldn't have stayed." Tears leaked from her eyes, but she did her best to ignore them and stay strong.

I took a step forward, testing the waters. Once I saw she was okay with it, I wrapped my arms around her and gave her a hug. "I'm sorry, Macy. I'm really sorry. If you want to, I think you should go back to Indianapolis. Do whatever will make you happy. You don't deserve friends like me."

Macy pulled back, wiping tears from her eyes. She opened her mouth to say something, but I shushed her.

I heard something.

"Kane, wh—"

I held my finger up and listened closely. A door creaked. A radio crackled.

"Someone's here," I whispered.

Macy looked at me like I was crazy. "Yeah, it's a school."

"Target in sight," someone whispered.

I looked to my right just in time to see a purple Eximus bolt flying right at me. I dropped to the ground and the bolt flew down the hallway and slammed into the trophy case. Glass exploded and fire alarms rang.

I grabbed Macy and dashed inside the closest classroom. The students yelled in surprise when they saw me suddenly appear.

"What the hell is going on?" the teacher yelled.

Macy jumped back, looking around, trying to figure out where she was and how she'd gotten there so fast.

"I'm sorry I didn't say anything sooner," I said as I turned to the teacher, Mr. Aspen. "Evacuate the school," was all I could tell him. Then I turned and dashed out of the classroom.

A wall of soldiers in black now stood on my right, each one holding an Eximus gun.

I turned to my left and began running down the hallway. Not as fast as I could, though. I wanted them to see where I was going.

Eximus charges flew all around me, but none made contact. I looked over my shoulder and saw that the soldiers were beginning to chase after me, just like I wanted.

I turned right down the hallway and picked up the pace a little bit. I braced myself and charged through the fire exit door at the end of the hallway. The soldiers had yet to make it around the corner, but they'd know to go through the destroyed doorway.

"*Kane Andrews,*" a voice boomed from a loudspeaker.

I stopped in my tracks and looked up. Helicopters were circling above me, each of them filled with soldiers. One of them had a camera pointed right at me, broadcasting to who knew where.

"*Surrender immediately. We have the place surrounded. There is no escape, Tempest.*"

This time I didn't need an Eximus blast to have all my strength taken from me. It left on its own accord.

They knew. They knew I was Tempest; that Tempest was me.

Macy knew. The kids in Mr. Aspen's classroom knew.

Whoever was watching the feed from that camera knew.

"Oh my god, Kane," Samantha said in my head. "It's all over the news. That camera is sending a feed to every station in America. The whole world knows you're Tempest."

I'd stood there for too long. Soldiers surrounded me, all pointing their guns at me. I looked up into the helicopter that held the camera. Sitting next to it was Loren, a giant smile spread across her face. She waved, looking more satisfied than anyone I'd ever seen in my life.

This was all just a show. Loren knew I'd be able to escape. The soldiers didn't shoot at me, even though they were standing in a circle around me. This was all just a power play.

I launched myself into the air, flying as fast as I could to Indianapolis. No matter how fast I flew, though, there was no escaping the fact that the whole world knew that I, Kane Andrews, was the superhero Tempest.

Chapter 42

Only the Beginning

I FLEW THROUGH THE front door of our apartment building and up the stairwell, coming to a stop at the front door of the apartment. I frantically grabbed my keys from my pocket and after a couple of tries, finally got the key in the lock. I burst into the apartment, slamming the door shut behind me.

Mom and Dad were standing in front of the TV, watching the news. They turned and saw me as I walked in. Mom rushed me and gave me a hug.

"Everything's going to be okay," she said.

I nodded and pulled away from her hug. "I know, but right now we need to get out of here. Pack your bags. They're probably on their way here right now."

Dad nodded. "I'll get all the cash from my safe. Zoe, you start packing."

The two of them rushed into their bedroom and I ran to mine. I grabbed a duffel bag from my closet and filled it with my clothes and toiletries in seconds. I grabbed another and ran to the closet that held my Tempest outfits. I shoved all of them into the bag and then put the two of them by the front door.

I walked over to the TV, watching what was happening in disbelief.

"We're on location at Ebon High School, where it was just revealed that senior Kane Andrews is, in fact, the superhuman Tempest," the blonde television reporter said. "This has been confirmed by Loren Westlake, director of a government division known as the Super Task Force. We are on location with Director Westlake now."

The camera zoomed out a bit and Loren stepped into the shot, that smug look of satisfaction still plastered on her face. "How are you, Melissa?"

"I'm good, thank you," the reporter said. "First of all, how did you learn the identity of Tempest?"

"Well, we've been working for months on figuring out the science behind the Supers and what we can do to protect the American people from them. We never want to have something like the Richter crisis again, and we won't. Part of the process was learning everything we could about Tempest. Then we just followed the clues until they led us here. Mr. Andrews demonstrated his abilities in his escape from the high school moments ago."

"Is that something you'd planned, his escape?"

"Yes, of course. We had to prove he was Tempest, and he did so magnificently. It won't be long before he's in our custody," Loren said, looking straight into the camera, knowing I would be watching.

My heart beat so fast I thought it would explode. I was freaking out. I had no idea what I was going to do. My life was over. I could never be Kane Andrews again. Everybody would know my face. Everybody on the planet would know who I was. *This is it. I'm through.*

"One of the questions I know is going to come up is why he should be taken into custody. I know this is going to spark major debate. Could you elaborate a little bit?"

"Yes, of course. It's clear that all Supers are a danger to society. Just look at Richter. He could've wiped us all out. Yes, Tempest—Kane—is the one who took him out. However, what people don't know is that Kane actually came to us for help. We're the ones who came up with the plan to stop Richter."

I almost threw my remote through the TV screen. It wasn't their plan at all! It wasn't my plan either, though; it was Samantha's. But she was on my team. On my side. Besides, Loren hadn't even answered the damn question! All she was trying to do was create some character assassination. She was trying to make me look weak.

It took all the power within me not to fly back to Ebon and argue my case. I didn't have time for that, though. I had to get my family to safety.

"Come to Los Angeles as soon as you can, Kane. We need to talk in person," Samantha said in my head.

"Yeah, don't worry, I'll be there," I said.

"Kane, are you ready? We need to leave," Dad said as he walked out of his bedroom.

"Yeah, I'm good to go," I said as I walked toward the door.

Dad handed me his and Mom's cell phones. "Destroy these."

I took the two phones in my hands and took out my anger and frustration on them. I crushed them as hard as I could; you couldn't even tell what they'd once been when I was done. Then I took my own phone out of my pocket and clicked on the screen. It was filled with missed calls and texts. A few of them were even from Macy. I crushed the phone in my hand, even though I wanted to stop and read what people were saying.

Having taken out some of my anger on the phones, I felt a bit better.

"Let's get out of here," Dad said.

The three of us walked out of our apartment, and I know we all felt the fear creeping in. I knew this was only the beginning.

CHAPTER 43

CALLED OUT

"DREW'S FAMILY WENT into hiding just in case, too. I'll fly him up when I'm done here," I told Samantha and Doug as I paced inside their storage unit.

"What are you going to do?" Samantha asked me again.

And again, I had no answer. I stopped pacing and stared at the wall. I honestly didn't have the slightest clue. What could I do? Everyone knew who I was. Everyone knew my face. I could never go out in public without my Tempest costume on again.

Okay, maybe that was a bit dramatic, but the point remained. For the second time in the past year, my life had changed forever. "I'm going to continue being Tempest," I said. "With Atlas and his Legion of Richter hiding in the shadows, waiting to strike, now's not the time to give up. It's just going to be impossible to be Kane Andrews."

"What about your parents?" Doug asked.

I sighed. I felt so guilty. Their lives were now ruined forever because of me. They would be less recognizable than I was, but Dad would never be able to practice law again, that was for sure. I had no idea what they were going to do. "I don't know, Doug."

"I can't get hold of Holocene. She was out all night trying to track down some info on Atlas," Samantha said with a frustrated grunt.

"She's going to be in for a surprise once she wakes up," I said.

"That's for sure," Samantha said, followed quickly by, "Holy shit."

"Oh, no, what is it?" I said, walking around her desk. I glanced at her computer screen and things went from bad to worse.

"We've just received this video from a superhuman named Atlas, leader of a gang known as the Legion of Richter. We're receiving reports from local law enforcement that Atlas and his gang have taken out the Super Task Force soldiers in the area and have taken hostages inside Ebon High School. In the video, he appears to be calling out Tempest, recently identified as seventeen-year-old Kane Andrews. Watch," the news reporter said.

The screen shifted to a shot of Atlas pointing a camera at himself. "Hello, Tempest. Or Kane. I'll have to find out which you prefer when I see you," he said. I could hear chuckles in the background. "It's been a few years since I've been in high school, but some things never change. Everybody has a group. A clique. Yours seems to have dwindled in the past few months. First your friend Michael is killed when you and Richter drop a roof on him—which, by the way, bravo. Then there was Drew, who I found out actually used to work for the STF. How crazy is that? Your own best friend, working for the enemy. Well, your clique is about to take another hit." The camera panned to the right and the shot rested on one of the people he had taken hostage: Macy.

She had been crying, but I had a feeling it wasn't out of fear of Atlas. She looked at him with strong, fierce eyes. She wasn't afraid. And I had a feeling it was because she knew that I'd save her, just like I had all those months ago when I'd first discovered my powers.

"Look here, it's the famous Macy Westling, the first person you saved. This is just too great. So poetic. Not only the first person you saved, but also your *ex*-girlfriend? I can't make this up, people!" Atlas turned the camera back to himself. "So, Tempest. Kane. Whatever. You'd better get down here to good ol' Ebon High, home of the fighting Eagles. I'd like to have that talk we were supposed to have in Oregon before you flew off on me. I really want to introduce myself, but I also really want to kill Little Miss Macy. So either you come say hi, or Macy's going to take a fall from the top of the high school auditorium, the place our father Richter dropped her. The place where it all began. You may be cowering in some seedy hotel room right now, so you might not have the news on at this moment. So I'll give you a little bit of time to see this. You have three hours. If you aren't here by then, Macy goes skydiving without a parachute. Then it's on to the next hostage..."

The camera cut off and the screen turned back to the reporter. It took her a few moments to gather her thoughts, and by the time she had, I was already on my way to Ebon.

Chapter 44
Introductions

I HOVERED OVER EBON High School, watching as the many news vans, police vehicles and helicopters circled the area.

"Kane, you should wait for Holocene," Samantha said.

"I can't, Samantha. I can do this. He just wants to talk. If anything goes bad, I can get Macy out of there and stay back until Holocene arrives," I told her.

"I don't know, Kane. I don't like this. You haven't even had time to think or process any of this."

"I don't have time, Samantha! Atlas is going to kill Macy. I don't have time to wait around and process my feelings." And the truth was, this was a welcome distraction. I wasn't sure how to be Kane Andrews anymore, but being Tempest was easy. "Stick around. I might need you," I said.

I flew down toward the auditorium. I landed at the front doors, then paused for a moment to make sure the cameras were on me. I wanted them to see that I was standing up to Atlas. I wasn't cowering away. I was going to save Macy and the rest of the hostages.

I was a hero.

I opened the door and walked in. I could only imagine how badly all the reporters were freaking out at that moment. I entered the large gym, the room that held so many memories.

In the center sat about thirty hostages, a mixture of faculty and students. They were all sitting on the floor except for Macy, who was sitting tied to a chair. Atlas was standing behind her, watching me as I walked in.

Four Supers were flying around the room, doing nothing but trying to look intimidating. There were six men in black uniforms holding Eximus blasters.

"Oh my gosh, it's worse than I thought. Are those non-Super human soldiers?" Samantha said.

I didn't respond, but I held the same suspicion.

"Ah, Kane Andrews. It's a pleasure," Atlas said as I got close. He extended his hand, but I didn't shake it.

"I'm here. Let her go," I said, looking at Macy. She looked up at me, fighting back a smile. She knew I'd save her, like I had what seemed like years ago, back in July.

"I'm a man of my word and will do so when we're through. We have some things to discuss first," Atlas said.

"I'm not discussing anything unless the hostages are free," I told him, my voice firm and confident. I wasn't going to budge.

Atlas made a gesture and the Supers who had been flying around the gym landed behind me. "You're in no position to negotiate, Kane."

"Call me Tempest," I said.

"I don't see you wearing your Tempest attire," Atlas said, looking me up and down. "All I see is some high schooler here to save his girlfriend."

I gritted my teeth, but said nothing in return. He was

right. I couldn't negotiate and I couldn't fight without putting Macy and the other hostages in danger. I started to realize that rushing in here might've been a mistake.

"I would like to tell you about the Legion of Richter," Atlas said as he clasped his hands together, his long fingers intertwining. "See if you'd be interested in joining."

"Why the hell would I join something called 'the Legion of Richter'? I killed Richter, in case you forgot," I said, trying to appear as tough as possible.

"Yes, of course. And for that I thank you. You see, when you killed Richter, he was no longer restrained by his human form. He was able to evolve to a higher plane of existence and he's chosen me as his messenger," Atlas said. He stood tall and proud, as if he were the most important person in the world. As if what he was saying were actually true.

"You really believe that?" I said. "I don't know if I'd be taking orders from someone who was so easy to kill."

Atlas laughed. "Richter isn't dead, Kane. I've already explained that. He has a plan for the world, a plan the two of us came up with together. A plan that can either include you, or exclude you. The choice is yours."

I stood there for a moment, waiting for more, but there was none. Atlas simply stood there, waiting for my answer. "Really? That's all you've got? You aren't going to give me any sort of idea what this plan is?"

One of the Supers behind me chuckled, but I ignored her.

"Kane—"

"Tempest."

"I'm not going to tell you. Not unless you join me. I will say that if you don't, I'll kill you. Very easily, too. While you were out gallivanting, I was studying. Learning. Richter taught me many things about my powers. I'm more powerful than you and him combined. I will kill you. I'll kill everyone you care about. I swear to you."

I shook my head and chuckled. "Do you know how I know you're crazy?"

Atlas smirked. "Please, enlighten me."

"If you really believed what you're saying about Richter, there's no way you'd be asking me to join you. I *killed* him."

"I will not stand for your blasphemy!" Atlas shouted. "You did Richter a favor! You released him!"

"No, I killed him!" I shouted back. I took a step forward. "Do you know what I think? You want me to join you, because you know that if I don't, I'll do everything in my power to stop you. You're afraid of me. Afraid I might beat you. That I might win. Well, let me tell you something, you piece of shit. I'm gonna kill you just like I killed your god."

Atlas slammed his fist into my chest, hitting harder than I'd even been hit before. I went flying backwards, right through the walls of the gymnasium. I heard Macy scream, but it sounded faint as I rocketed through the parking lot of the school.

I slammed into a line of parked cars, sending all five of them up in a fiery explosion. People screamed as they fled and camera crews zoomed in, ready to catch the action.

I stood up, my body already beginning to heal itself. I walked out of the flames and pulled the burning clothes off me, revealing the Tempest outfit I had been secretly wearing underneath. I pulled the hood up and my eyes began to glow. I rocketed back through the parking lot and flew through the hole I'd made in the wall on the way out.

I landed, sliding across the wooden gym floor. The hostages began cheering, but Atlas' crew shushed them.

Atlas cocked his head to the side as he examined me. "All right, then. Let's see what Tempest is made of."

Chapter 45
Full Circle

ATLAS' CREW CHARGED at me all at once. I jumped over their heads quickly and kicked the guy in the middle hard in the back. He rocketed into the wall, but didn't go through. He slammed into it, groaning in pain. These guys weren't as strong as I was, it seemed.

The girl who had laughed at me earlier was faster than the others. She turned around and reached me in seconds. She swung once, but I ducked beneath her punch. She was ready for that, though, and her next punch was low. Her fist slammed into my face and I stumbled sideways.

She came at me swinging, but I dodged her and she missed. She stumbled forward and I used her momentum to grab her wrist and swing her around. I threw her through the backboard of one of the basketball nets. Glass exploded everywhere and she hung tangled in the twisted metal of the net.

One of the other guys charged at me again, but I went on the offensive. I leaped at him, slamming him backwards, then grabbed his shirt and flew upwards. I slammed him into the ceiling and then swung him in the air, slamming him into the wall again. I threw him into the lighting system of the gym, causing the lights to explode and electricity to course through him. The lights flickered and the man fell thirty feet to the ground in a smoking crater.

A bolt of Eximus exploded next to me. Atlas' soldiers had begun shooting at me. Atlas was getting worried.

I flew down to the soldiers and extended my arm. I flew past their feet, hitting them with my arm. They were knocked in the air and fell to the ground in a heap. I picked up the gun from the last guy in the line, turned around and shot all of them. They seized as the electricity flowed through them, knocking them unconscious.

One of Atlas' guys wrapped his arms around me from behind, sending me tumbling into the wall next to me. I tried to get him off me, but he was holding on too tight. He tried to take the gun from my hands, but I kept a firm grip. Almost too firm, as I felt the handle of the gun begin to bend beneath my hands.

The struggling caused me to hit the trigger, sending bolts of Eximus all over the room. People screamed as they dodged the blasts. I was able to get my elbow loose enough that I could slam it into my attacker's stomach. He went flying backwards off me, and I turned around in mid-air. I fired two bolts into him as he tumbled backwards. He fell to the ground in an electrified heap.

I turned to face Atlas, who was fuming with anger at the failures of his goons. I aimed the Eximus gun at him and fired a handful of bolts at him, but he saw them coming. He dodged them with ease.

He leaped through the air and before I knew it, he slammed me into the ground, his foot on top of me holding me down. I grabbed his ankle to throw him off me, but when I pushed against it he didn't budge.

That's impossible, I thought. I struggled against him, pushing his leg, wiggling beneath his grasp, doing everything I could to escape. Nothing worked.

He was too strong. Way stronger than I was.

"How are you…" I tried to finish the sentence, but I couldn't get the words out. I was struggling too hard.

"You were the second person to become a Super, yet you're still so naïve," Atlas said, as calm as he could be. "You'll pay for this. The end will begin the same way the beginning did, with Macy Westling falling from the rooftop."

Atlas took his foot off me and dashed to Macy, grabbed her, and disappeared outside the building.

I jumped up and ran outside as fast as I could. I looked up and saw Atlas standing at the edge of the Ebon High gymnasium roof, holding Macy over the edge by her throat.

He let her go.

I jumped up to catch her, exactly as I had all those months ago, moving so fast she fell in slow motion. But Atlas didn't.

Atlas slammed into me, knocking me away from Macy. I wasn't going to let him stop me. Before he could pin me to the ground, I flew out from beneath his feet. Macy inched to the ground, all in painfully slow motion. I reached out for her, felt her red hair between my fingers.

Atlas tackled me, sending the two of us flying through the gymnasium. We exited out the back wall and I got out of his grip. I flew over the rooftop and saw Macy as she reached the halfway point.

I flew down, but Atlas got hold of me again. He grabbed me and threw me straight down to the ground, right through the roof of the gymnasium. I caught myself before I hit the ground and redirected my flight path.

I flew out through the wall, bricks freezing in the air as the wall exploded around me. I stood right beneath Macy. I could almost reach up to grab her.

Atlas came at me one last time. He grabbed me and began to fly along the wall of the gym, holding me out in front of him the whole way. My body slammed into the wall nonstop. The pain was immense, but I ignored it. I had to save Macy.

Atlas was angry, and that meant he was sloppy. His grip wasn't tight enough on me and he was leaning a little too far forward. I placed my foot on his chest and using his momentum, threw him off me, far into the air.

I flew to Macy just in time. I wrapped my arms around her, slowing her descent. Time sped up back to normal as I slowed down. I shielded Macy with my body as the gymnasium fell to the ground behind us, unable to stand after the beating Atlas and I had put on it in a matter of seconds.

After the dust and debris had settled, I stood, helping Macy up. "You okay?" I asked.

She wrapped her arms around me. "I don't know what to say. Thank you."

I smiled as we let go. "No problem. All part of my job."

Macy smiled and was about to say something else, but four gunshots rang out.

Four bullet holes appeared in Macy's chest.

I caught her before she fell to the ground, but she was dead before I even laid a finger on her.

"I was trying to be poetic, but I guess I'll stick to just getting the job done from now on." Atlas threw aside the pistol he'd used to kill Macy. "See you soon, Kane," he said, then launched himself into the air.

I didn't follow. I couldn't. I was numb. I let out a blood-curdling scream that shattered the windows of all the cars around me.

I didn't want it to be true. It couldn't be. But as I looked down at her lifeless body, I couldn't deny it.

Macy was dead, and there was nothing I could do to save her.

Chapter 46
Clouded Judgment

IT WAS COLD on the night Macy died as I waited on a rooftop in Dallas for Holocene.

I still couldn't believe she was dead, and it was all because of me. Because they'd found out who Tempest was. This was exactly what I'd worked so hard to avoid. I didn't even know how they'd been able to figure out who I was, but that didn't matter anymore. All that mattered now was that I stopped Atlas. I needed to keep my mind off everything. I didn't want to think. I didn't want to process. I just wanted to fight.

Holocene landed on the rooftop five minutes after we were supposed to meet.

"You're late," I said.

"Sorry about that," she said, brushing her brown hair behind her ear. "I was a little busy. I'm sorry about your friend. Well, everything, really. I should've been there."

Yeah, you should've, I thought. I didn't want to think about the fact that Samantha had told me to wait. That maybe if I'd listened and waited for Holocene, Macy would still be alive. Atlas wouldn't have gotten away. Maybe—there I went. Thinking about it. "What do you know about Atlas and the Legion? Samantha said you were out last night chasing some leads."

Holocene hesitated and crossed her arms. "Are you sure you want to do this? You don't want to talk or anything?"

"No, Holocene, I don't," I snapped.

"Tempest, you're upset right now. You need some time. We all understand that. You've been through a lot," she said, taking a step forward.

I shrank back. "I don't want time. Time is the last thing I have to waste. I spent six months in a coma on the moon, for chrissakes. 'Taking time' is the last thing I want to do!" I yelled.

"Okay, Tempest, you need to quiet down," Holocene said, raising her hands to calm me. She took a couple more steps forward. It was like she was approaching a cornered feral animal.

"I am calm! I'm very calm!" I yelled. "I just want to understand why, when I'm trying to stop Atlas and the army he's building, you're telling me to calm down! To take some time off! I don't need. Any. Time. I just want to find Atlas!"

"Tempest, it's okay to admit that you're in pain. It's okay to admit that you failed. I-uh—" Holocene said, quickly trying to recover.

It was too late. The words had already come out.

You failed.

"Oh, so you think I'm just a screw-up now, don't you?" I snapped, taking a step forward. "You just want me to stay out of your way so you can take out Atlas by yourself, don't you? You think you're just going to swoop in and finish what I started? You think you're better than me, and you think I'll just slow you down, don't you?"

"Of course not!" Holocene shouted back. "We're a team, Tempest! We're going to take down Atlas. You, me, Samantha, Doug, the people I recruited while you were captured. All of us together!"

Anger and frustration grew within me. I felt waves of anger slamming against the shores of my brain. I couldn't think clearly. All I wanted to do was take it out on Atlas. "If you won't tell me where they're at, I'll fly up and down the entire country until I find him myself!"

I launched myself into the air with such force that a small crater formed in the ground beneath me and flew toward the East Coast. I planned on flying up and down, working my way west until I saw Atlas or he saw me.

Just outside of Dallas, Holocene flew in front of me and stopped. I came to a halt a foot or two away. "Get out of my way!"

"Tempest, don't do this. You can't take him alone."

"I don't want to, but you aren't helping me!"

"You need time! Take just a day to process."

I flew past her. I didn't need her to tell me what to do.

Holocene grabbed my arm as I flew by and threw me to the ground. I slammed down through some trees and landed on the floor of the woods. Holocene stood over me, pinning me down.

I pushed my feet up against her chest and threw her off me. She slammed into some trees, knocking them to the ground. I dodged out of their way and jumped up into the air.

The trunk of a tree slammed into me, sending me flying through the woods, slicing through trees as I flew. I slowed and came to a stop, falling to the ground.

Holocene flew toward me, her hand in a fist. I rolled out

of the way and she punched the ground, sending a geyser of dirt into the air. "Tempest, stop it!" she yelled. "I don't want to fight you!"

I swung at her, my punch sloppy. She easily dodged it. I wasn't sure why I wanted to fight her so bad, but I had to take all my emotions out on somebody.

Holocene slammed her fist into the lower part of my back and I fell to my knees. She got behind me and put me in a headlock. "Stop fighting, Tempest. Just stop this."

I struggled against her grasp, but it was half-hearted. Even though she had me in a headlock, feeling someone put their arms around me struck a certain chord within me. I realized that Holocene was fighting me because she cared about me. She didn't want me to go out there and do something I'd regret. If anybody could kill me, Atlas could. None of us knew for sure, but we didn't want to find out.

Holocene just wanted me to get better.

I relaxed. I stopped fighting and collapsed into Holocene's grasp. The moonlight filtered through the treetops as she held me on the forest floor. "I failed. Macy died because I failed. I should've waited for you. I should've waited," I said, crying.

"Shh, it's okay. It'll be okay. Atlas will pay for what he did. I promise you. He'll pay."

I nodded reluctantly. "We'll do it together, Holocene."

"Selena," she said.

I looked up at her, confused.

She pulled off her mask, revealing her entire face. "My name is Selena."

"It's nice to meet you, Selena. My name is Kane," I said.

I began to laugh and soon Selena did as well. My tears turned to laughter as my emotions poured out of me.

Chapter 47
The Siege Begins

TWO DAYS LATER, I was sitting in my favorite chair in the storage unit as Selena explained what she knew about Atlas and the Legion. Samantha and Doug were there, as was a super with flight and strength called Nep. He was the dark-skinned guy who had come with Selena to rescue me from the STF. He wasn't wearing any sort of mask or costume. I wasn't sure where the girl who had been with them was. Hank and Drew were both there, though. It felt especially nice having Drew there.

Basically, it was really cramped and really hot in there.

"I think Atlas himself is in Washington D.C., as that's where some of the more evil Supers have been congregating. Even reports of that teleporter Kane and I took down have popped up."

"Ugh, Sven," I groaned.

"That guy's the worst," Hank said.

"Anyway, that's the most logical place for him to be," Selena said.

"I don't like the idea of Atlas and his Legion hiding out in the nation's capital," Drew said.

I nodded in agreement. "Whatever he's planning, it can't be good."

"I think he's planning something in more than just those cities, though," Selena said. She turned to Nep, who stood up straight.

"I was patrolling New York City and ran into some guys who were flying around the *R* those bastards engraved into the Statue of Liberty. They fled when I got close, but I caught one of them. They kept saying the word 'mark' over and over again, like some sort of crazy person. I thought it was a name—"

"—but he meant a mark as in a *target*?" Samantha said, interrupting him.

Nep nodded. "Exactly. All the *R's* are marking their territory—territory they're going to want to take soon."

"Where are the *R's* all at?" Hank asked.

"New York City, Dallas, Chicago, Los Angeles, and D.C.," Selena replied.

I sighed and slumped back into my seat. That was a lot of cities, and there weren't a lot of us. From what I gathered from the word *legion* in the Legion of Richter, Atlas had a lot of people on his side. People *and* Supers, from what it seemed. And plenty of Eximus guns from the raid on the STF complex. This was going to be very difficult.

"Okay, so I'll keep watch on Dallas, of course," Selena said. "Nep's got New York. Drew and Hank, no offense, but you won't be able to watch a whole city on your own."

"None taken," Drew said.

"I'm not that stretchy," Hank agreed.

"Hank, I think you should go with Nep. Drew, you're with Kane. You guys will watch L.A."

Drew and I made eye contact, giving each other a nod and a smile. I was really excited to work with him. He was my best friend, and we were superheroes together. It didn't get much better than that.

"What about us?" Doug asked.

"We'll stay here and keep an eye on all news reports, police scanners, everything we can get our hands on," Samantha said. "I'll report it to everyone out in the field. We'll also keep an extra close eye on the cities we don't have anyone in, like Chicago and D.C., so if anything goes wrong we'll be able to direct whoever's not busy there."

"Are you sure there's not something that needs to be hacked? Because if there is, I can hack it," Doug said.

I chuckled. "Yes Doug, we know. We aren't fighting robots, though."

"Never say never," Doug said under his breath.

I rolled my eyes.

"I have a few more things I want to go over before we get going," Selena began.

"Yeah, you might want to save that," Samantha said. She pointed at something on her screen. "Local news stations here in L.A. are reporting that Supers just tore down the statue of Kane at the USC campus."

Thank god.

"I got reports of some Supers destroying some construction sites in New York," Doug said, tapping on his keyboard.

I stood up from my chair and flipped up the hood on my Tempest uniform. "Everybody get to your cities. It's beginning."

*

I dropped Hank and Drew off in the middle of the USC campus. The Supers there didn't have powers that were too crazy, so I figured they'd be able to take them out easily. Then I turned north up to Koreatown, where one of the more powerful Supers was wreaking havoc.

Before I got there I could see a car fly high into the air and had déjà vu back to the times of Richter. I landed on the street a few hundred feet from the Super.

My heart was pumping and my adrenaline rushed. I was ready.

The Super loomed about seven or eight feet tall. He was huge, his muscles bulging all over. He looked more monster than man as he tossed a car at a crowd of pedestrians who were trying to run away.

I caught the car right before it got to them. I swung it around and launched it right back at the Super. The car slammed into him and he stumbled backwards. He was thrown off by my attack, and let out a roar in anger.

"Are you seeing this, Samantha?" I asked.

"Yeah, he's all over the news. What is it?" she asked.

I grabbed another car he threw my way, tossing it back at him like a Super version of catch. "I don't know! He's strong, though. He looks like some sort of experiment gone wrong."

"I'll see what I can find later. Gotta help Selena. Two of the Supers at Ebon High are playing hide and seek with her in downtown Dallas," Samantha said before leaving my mind.

Things really were beginning to kick off.

A fire truck slammed into me, sending me flying into the building behind me. I hadn't seen that one coming. I crashed through the glass walls of the building and slid through a row of empty cubicles, sure that the fire truck would destroy everything after me.

We slid to a halt and I placed my feet on the grill of the

truck. I gave it a hard push and sent it shooting back out the building. I flew after it, making sure it had the right trajectory.

It did, and it slammed into the back of the Super, smashing him to the ground. The Super let out a guttural roar as he pushed the fire engine off him, sending it high into the air before it landed on the top of a nearby building.

I rushed the Super, pounding my fist into its chest. The Super flew backward a foot or two, but not nearly as far as another Super or human would've flown.

I hadn't been expecting this, so when the monster Super quickly recovered and hammered his large fist into my side, I went shooting down the street. Pain filled my body as I tried to slow myself down. I was aided by the three-hundred-thousand-dollar sports car I careened into, destroying it.

I climbed out of the wreckage. The Super charged down the street at me on all fours. "Where the hell did this thing come from?" I asked myself. He looked like a monster you'd see on some late night TV show, but was clearly human, based on his human face and form.

I jumped over his head as he got close and he skidded across the ground, stumbling over himself to try to bring himself to a stop. He began to turn himself around to come back for a second pass, but I was right in his face before he could do so.

I delivered a Super-punch to his right cheek, causing his body to fly up and twist in the air. Then I brought my fist down into his chest, sending his hulking body into the ground hard, creating a crater in the road. The Super was dazed, but tried to get up. I slipped my hands beneath his body and lifted him into the air.

I flew up fast and high. The Super struggled, trying to get

free, but I kept a tight grip on him. Once I was high above the city, I turned around and threw him at the ground.

The creature-like Super rocketed toward the ground, wailing in the air trying to grab hold of something. I flew down toward it, my fist extended, ready to seal the deal and smash him into the ground.

A blur came out of nowhere to the left. This new Super swooped in and grabbed the creature, flying off into the distance with him.

I slowed myself and came to a halt a few feet from the ground. I took in the destroyed street. Destroyed cars burned all around, filling the air with the smell of burning gasoline. The fire engine's sirens wailed a warped tune, while people peeked out the windows of the damaged building, checking to see if the Super was gone.

That thing had really done a number on this area, and there'd been no reason for him to do so. He'd been destroying stuff just for the sake of destroying it.

I waited a few more moments, making sure that that creature-Super wasn't going to come back. He seemed to be gone for good, taken away by whoever that other Super was who had caught him. I didn't like what the existence of that *thing* implied. I had a feeling we had no idea what we were actually up against.

I left the street and flew back to the USC campus. I landed just in time to see Hank trip a guy who was charging at Drew. Drew punched the falling Super with his arms, which were surging with Eximus energy, and the Super crumpled to the ground in a seizing heap.

"You got this under control?" I shouted.

Drew and Hank looked up at me, nodding. "Most fun I've had in a long time!" Drew shouted up at me with a laugh.

"Kane, get to Dallas as soon as you can. Selena could use your help with the two Supers she's dealing with. She's holding her own, but things could turn ugly quick," Samantha said in my head.

"Gotta run, guys. Stay safe!" I told them.

"Will do!" Hank shouted up at me. Then the two of them ran off, looking for any more members of the Legion of Richter who needed to be dealt with.

I turned and flew through the air, heading toward Dallas. It was time to see what kind of trouble Selena had gotten herself into.

CHAPTER 48
TAG TEAM

AS I GOT close to Klyde Warren Park in downtown Dallas, I saw a female Super grab Selena by the hair and throw her through the air. The other Super—an Asian teen—hit her in the air, slamming her to the ground.

Things didn't seem to be going her way at all.

The female charged at Selena as she climbed off the ground. She was about to hit her, but I got there first. I flew into the girl, tackling her in the air. We tumbled across the ground, sending grass and dirt flying around us.

We came to a halt and I grabbed the girl's shirt. I threw her backward over my head, hoping Selena would crash into her just like that guy had, but a quick glance showed me that Selena was busy fighting said guy.

The girl was able right herself in the air before I had the chance to realize what se was doing, and she struck me in the chest, sending me backward. She didn't stop there, though. She kept flying with me, keeping her foot square on my chest, pushing me backward.

I struck a nearby office building, flying through each wall with explosive force, the Super right on top of me. We came out the other end, and I was able to regain my composure. I grabbed the girl's foot and pushed it down toward the ground. Her momentum kept her going forward, though, and she tumbled to the ground, head over heels.

I slowed myself and pulled a light pole up from the ground. The female Super stood up, a bit dazed and confused. I put the light pole over my shoulder like a bat and swung at the Super as hard as I could. She went flying through the air, back toward the park.

I jumped into the air, following the Super. As she reached the park, Selena flew into the air and grabbed her, then threw her to the ground hard.

I landed next to the two of them as Selena pulled the female Super up and began beating on her.

I could hear the Asian Super running up behind me to sucker punch me, and I dodged out of the way just in time. I grabbed his fist as it soared above my head and redirected his momentum straight into the ground. Then I got on top of him and began hitting him in the face as hard as I could.

I got three punches in before I felt an immense pain hit my back, sending me straight to the ground. Not only was the pain immense, it was terrifying. The humming feeling of the Eximus coursed through my brain, removing my ability to use my powers.

STF soldiers were surrounding the park, firing their Eximus guns at us. I tried my best to move, but even though the pain was subsiding, I was paralyzed for a few more moments.

Selena ran to my side and grabbed me. She jumped into the air and I watched as the park got smaller and smaller below us. Wave after wave of Eximus blasts slammed into the two

Legion members who still hadn't fully recovered from my and Selena's beating.

I felt my powers returning and was able to stand when Selena dropped me off on the rooftop of a building.

"Looked like you could use the help," she said as she put her hands on her knees, taking deep breaths.

"Same goes for you," I said with labored breathing, each breath returning more and more of my power.

"Got some activity in downtown Chicago," Samantha said. "Three Supers fighting the STF. Some casualties have been reported."

I looked at Selena and she at me. "You get that?" I said.

She nodded.

"Well, then, let's go," I said, and we launched into the air, flying toward Chicago.

The fact that there were so many STF soldiers around troubled me. The organization must've been bigger than I'd thought, and with the Legion attacking, it was only going to make Loren look more and more like a hero in the public eye. In a way, I guessed she was. We shared a common enemy. But we were enemies as well, so I wasn't sure if that mattered much.

We reached Chicago in minutes and followed the screams.

We flew to the street the Supers were fighting on just in time to see them drop four STF soldiers from four stories up. "Go right!" I shouted at Selena.

I flew to the two on the left, catching one in each arm just in time. Then I flew them back to the line of STF soldiers, who had their guns raised, ready to shoot us.

I paid them no attention as I turned to the three Supers, who were very angry we were there to ruin their fun. I also tried to ignore the fact that I'd been able to catch those STF soldiers, but I couldn't save Macy. It stuck in my mind, though and I couldn't dislodge that fact. I thought I'd spent enough time processing and coming to terms with it, but it just came and hit me like a truck.

Then a Super came and hit me like a Super.

He hit me square in the face, but I didn't fly backward like I had with the others. This one wasn't nearly as strong. He swung at me again, and I dodged, but was surprised to find that his next punch landed as well. He made up in speed what he lacked in strength.

But what would take him twenty punches only took me one.

I reared back and slammed my fist into his face. He rocketed backwards, crashing into a glass-walled bus stop. He wasn't going to wake up for a while, that's for sure.

I looked up and saw Selena was getting her ass handed to her by the two other Supers. Feeling a sense of déjà vu, I flew down to the STF soldiers who were watching us, unsure of what to do. They didn't seem to want to fire, afraid they'd hit Selena and me, who'd just saved four of their own and seemed to be fighting the same people they were.

I reached out to a soldier at the front. "Give me your gun," I demanded.

He gave it to me without hesitation and I flew up to the Supers. I pulled the gun up to my shoulder and fired two blasts into the male Super. He fell to the ground and the STF was on him in a heartbeat. The only one left was a girl Super, who was ready for my shots.

I fired three blasts, but she dodged them easily. She lunged at me, but was jerked back by Selena grabbing her neck. Selena wrapped her arms around her, holding her tight.

I fired a blast right into her chest and Selena let her go. She fell to the ground, the Eximus energy zapping her powers.

I flew down and dropped the Eximus gun down next to her unconscious body just before the STF reached her.

Selena and I flew off before the STF soldiers could change their minds about attacking us or receive explicit orders to do so.

"Anything else, Samantha?" I said once Selena and I were hovering high above the city.

"No, it looks to me like everybody's got everything under con—oh god," Samantha exclaimed.

"What is it?" I shouted.

"Kane, Atlas himself is in Ebon. He's destroying the entire city," Samantha breathed. "I'm picking up more Supers right there in Chicago, too."

"I got Ebon, you take Chicago," I told Selena.

She opened her mouth to protest, but before she could, I rocketed toward Ebon. Nobody messes with my hometown.

Chapter 49
Home Field Disadvantage

I FLEW TO THE center of Ebon just in time to see Atlas rocket out the other side of the Ebon hospital.

I aimed directly for him, slamming into his body before he could reach the next building. Atlas and I tumbled toward the ground, landing in the middle of the street in a heap. Our impact sent cracks webbing out into the street. A water line cracked, sending a geyser of water into the air.

"Have you come for front row seats to the destruction of your hometown?" Atlas asked, raising his hands around him.

I said nothing. The last time I'd seen Atlas, he'd killed Macy. I didn't have the need or desire to talk.

I let out a yell and charged for him, getting one solid punch in to his face, sending him stumbling backward.

He swung back at me and I leaned back out of the way, his punch gliding right over my face.

I cocked my arm back, about to unleash a fury of attacks, but Atlas was quicker. He landed a solid blow into my chest, sending me rocketing into a car. The car exploded on impact, taking out the front of the store it was parked in front of.

Atlas jumped onto the burning car, standing over me in

the flames. He grabbed me and threw me out of the wreckage, sliding across the street. The water raining down from the burst main extinguished any flames on both me and Atlas.

"You think you're a match against me, Tempest?" Atlas said with a laugh.

I jumped up and charged at him, putting my shoulder down. He braced for my impact and as soon as I hit him, he grabbed me and threw me behind him. I flew through the front of a convenience store, taking out racks of snacks, flying through the selection of drinks and slamming into the dumpster in the back. I pushed myself up from the mangled dumpster, feeling lightheaded from my beating.

Atlas landed in front of me from nowhere and grabbed my throat. A look of evil washed over his face. A look of hatred. He squeezed my throat tight, cutting off my breathing. I couldn't get any oxygen. I punched at his hands, trying to get him to let go of me. But it was no use. He was much, much stronger than I was. I gasped for air, but none would come.

"You'll see," Atlas said as my vision faded. "You will pay."

I punched him once more in the chest, but I was weak and he was too strong. It did nothing.

Atlas produced a device that was charged with Eximus energy. I tensed, unsure of what he was about to do.

I didn't stay awake long enough to find out.

Chapter 50
Red Steps

THE MUFFLED SOUNDS of a man shouting with a crowd cheering in the background reached my ears. I felt a tired pain through my entire body. The pain in my head was a dull roar, washing over every inch of it.

A hum.

Eximus.

My fingers drifted to the back of my neck, and I could feel a hum of energy at the spot where my Eximus generator was implanted. I cursed under my breath. A new one had been implanted, and my powers were gone.

I realized I had yet to open my eyes. I tried to crack them open, but the process was painful. I got them open, but it wasn't much use. I was in some sort of cage, covered with a brown blanket. The cage was small, for a human at least. It seemed to be a dog cage big enough for a Great Dane. I got off my back and crouched.

"...We will not be hunted!"

Slice. Gurgling. Cheers.

"We will not be afraid, shamed into not living up to our full potential!"

Slice. Gurgling. Cheers.

"We were meant to be in charge! Do you want someone in power who isn't the maximum a human can be? More than human? A *super*human?"

Cheers.

"Fret no longer. We will take this country, little by little. We will make America free again!"

Slice. Gurgling. Cheers.

"Once we are finished with America, we will move on to the rest of the world! No one can stand in our way! And you, my people, will never want for anything. You will be taken care of. You will be kings and queens in a world filled with princes and princesses!"

Cheers. Slice. Gurgling. Cheers.

"But there are those who wish to stand in our way—"

Boos.

"—Those who wish to keep the world as it is. Those who don't realize that with this great leap in human evolution, there is no need for an evolution of society. Take Mr. Kane Andrews, for example."

The blanket was ripped from the cage and light flooded into my eyes. It took a moment for them to adjust, but once they had, I wanted nothing more than to have that blanket back.

A sea of people stretched out before me. They all shouted and booed at me, throwing things like rocks and water bottles, although none of it reached me.

I looked to my left and saw one of the most horrific sights I'd ever seen. Bodies lay with their heads hanging off the tops of some steps, their faces turned to the sky and blood pouring from their necks. The crimson blood ran down the many steps, dripping into a puddle at the bottom.

I looked behind me and saw the Lincoln Memorial. A giant marble Abraham Lincoln sat in his enormous chair, looking out at the Washington Monument. Again I looked down at the dead bodies and recognized one of them. It was that of President Martin. Next to him lay the vice president. My mouth dropped as I realized that all the dead bodies next to me were government officials. Politicians. Anybody who had had any power in the United States government lay next to me dead.

Atlas went on preaching to his crowd. His sea of hundreds of thousands, maybe even millions. Some of them were his human soldiers, other his Supers. Some of them were just humans who believed in following him and his Legion. Whether or not it was out of fear, or because they actually believed in his cause, I didn't know. All I knew was that every single person out there had stood there and watched while Atlas killed the entire United States government and they all seemed pleased about it.

"...and he thinks he's doing the American people—you," Atlas said, pointing to a camera. I realized there were cameras all over, transmitting his speech to viewers all over the world. People at home were watching while the United States died. "—a favor!" Atlas turned to me and got right up to my cage door. A grin covered his face. He held a microphone up to his mouth. "Isn't that right, Tempest? Are you doing these people a favor by holding them back? By not allowing those who deserve to rule the freedom to do so?"

He put the microphone up to my cage door, the sound of it hitting the metal echoing out of the speakers. I said nothing.

I just looked into Atlas' dark, evil eyes. And for a moment, I was frightened.

Atlas turned around to face his followers. "Good point, Tempest. Don't you agree, everybody? Maybe you all should follow him instead. He puts up a great argument."

The crowd laughed. They were laughing at *me*. Someone who had saved each and every one of their lives less than a year ago, they were now laughing at. Crazy how short their attention span was. All they cared about was that someone was in front of them, putting on a show. Making the most noise. Being the loudest voice in a sea of loud voices. They didn't care about the fact that he was murdering people right in front of them; all they cared about was whatever empty promises Atlas made them. At least for some, that was the case. Others were just afraid. To them it seemed like Atlas had already won, and if they didn't join him, they'd be dead.

Well, no matter what they thought, Atlas hadn't won. Things were far from over. They were just getting started.

"He thinks he's powerful, doesn't he?" Atlas said. He turned around and kicked my cage, sending it flying backward. It skidded across the marble floor until I was right underneath the feet of Abraham Lincoln.

The crowd cheered as Atlas floated through the air toward me. I grabbed my head, feeling blood coming from it. Atlas grabbed the front of the cage and tossed it behind him. Again I slid across the ground, this time until I reached the stairs and began tumbling down them, my whole body slamming around the cage. I felt one of my ribs crack, and the pain shot through me with every breath and tumble I took.

The crowd's cheering reached a fever pitch as I landed at the foot of the stairs. Supers were keeping the crowd back, but

I could see a few try to get over them, wanting to take a crack at my cage. I couldn't believe what I was seeing. It was total anarchy.

Atlas flew down to my cage and dragged me behind him as he walked back up to the top. The cage bounced up and down on the bloody steps, sending shocks of pain throughout my body. I tried to hold back tears. The whole world was falling apart around me. I was being humiliated and the people loved it. The blood that surrounded me had come from the people who had had control. When Atlas killed them, all that power had transferred to him. Now he was the most powerful Super, the leader of an army, and had control over the most powerful country in the world.

I looked at the face of the dead president. No number of Secret Service agents could've saved him. He'd been powerless to stop Atlas and his Legion. And at that moment, so was I.

Atlas reached the top of the stairs, bent down, and ripped off the front of my cage. He lifted it and shook me out of it. I fell to the ground in a heap, trying to keep gasps of pain from escaping my throat.

The crowd cheered.

"Here is your hero! Here is your Tempest!" Atlas shouted.

The crowd booed.

"Watch as he suffers the fate of your former leaders. No one can stand before me. No one!" Atlas screamed.

The crowd cheered.

Atlas produced a sword from inside the long jacket he was wearing. The sword crackled with Eximus energy, the hilt of it looking like some sort of steam punk, Frankenstein's monster creation.

I wasn't sure if I could be killed, but I didn't have my

powers at the moment, so if anything could kill me, it was that Eximus sword.

Atlas threw me down, my head hanging off the steps. He planted his foot on my chest. It felt like a giant anvil had been thrown onto me.

"You should've joined me, Kane. You should've listened," Atlas said, away from the microphone.

I said nothing back. I just stared into his crazy, hate-filled eyes with hate-filled eyes of my own. I wanted nothing more than to kill him in that moment. To end his reign of terror before it began. But I couldn't. I was powerless.

Atlas raised his sword, going for decapitation instead of throat slicing. I didn't close my eyes. I didn't wince. I showed no fear.

A gust of wind blew over me, causing my hair to whip about. Atlas looked around to see what was going on. Then he flew backward, having been thrown by someone.

Selena stood there in her Holocene gear, having just thrown Atlas back a couple of feet. Not far, but far enough. The crowd booed as she reached down to grab me. She jumped into the air and we flew off, away from the crowd. Away from the Legion of Richter.

"What took you so long?" I shouted in order to be heard over the wind.

"I had to take care of a couple of things first. Besides, I wanted to be a little dramatic," she said with a laugh.

"Where are we going?"

"Dallas. I've gathered everybody there," she said.

"What for?" I asked.

"Because in just a few hours, the Legion is going to launch a full-scale attack on the city."

CHAPTER 51
REGROUP

DREW FRIED MY Eximus generator and I felt my powers return. That was one of the greatest feelings ever, although it was one I didn't care to experience again, given the circumstances I had to be in to feel it.

I looked around the large office we had gathered in, situated on the 34th floor of one of the skyscrapers in downtown Dallas. Nobody was at work, or even outside of their homes, giving us full access to any building and office we wanted. Everybody was too scared to come out. They were all glued to their couches, all their attention on their TVs, watching the murders of our leaders along with society as we knew it.

Samantha was sitting behind the big mahogany desk, typing away on her laptop, tracking all the news flooding in from all over the country: the news that the Legion was taking over all the major cities, killing government officials and inserting themselves into power. They were turning the entire country into a tyranny and there wasn't anything anyone could do about it. No one but us.

Doug was sitting at the end of the desk, typing on his own laptop. Hank was standing next to him, leaning against the desk. Nep stood looking out the window at what was now a ghost town. Drew grabbed a bottled water from the mini fridge and Selena was standing across from me. I lay down on the large leather couch that sat in the corner of the office.

"How long was I gone?" I asked.

"Just a day. They kept you hidden so we were unable to find you," Selena said.

"So what do you know about this attack?" I asked as I sat up.

Selena sighed, trying to figure out where to begin. "Well, this was the only city we were able to completely drive the Legion away from. Of course, they *really* want to take it from us. Their Supers are flying in their soldiers from D.C. and are gathering them outside the city. It looks as if they'll be ready to attack in the next couple of hours."

I couldn't believe what I was hearing. It was beginning to dawn on me that this really was turning into an all-out war, and there were only seven of us defending the city. "Where's the STF?" I asked.

"A lot of them are dead," Selena said. "Those who aren't are either surrendering and joining the Legion, or doing what the rest of the population is doing and hiding."

"Shit," I breathed. We really were completely on our own. "So, what's the plan?"

"Honestly?" Samantha said, peeking over the top of her computer screen. "We really don't have one. None of us has the slightest clue what we're doing. Atlas must have some sort of military background, or at least his people do. They've got tanks, missile launchers, guns of both the bullet and Eximus variety—everything you'd need to launch an invasion of the city. I don't know how much of a chance we stand."

Hearing her say that discouraged me more than anything. Samantha had always had a plan. She had always been optimistic. Now? Nothing. She was accepting defeat.

"We stand at least a small chance, and that's enough for me," I said.

"How? How do we stand even a small one?" Samantha asked. "He has an army at our doorstep, armed with guns that are *designed* to take away our powers! No matter how fast you are, you can't run away from every single bolt of Eximus energy. We know that for a fact. Besides, if Atlas decides to show up, it'll really be over then. I just don't see an outcome where we come out on top."

I hated to admit it, but I was beginning to think she was right. Even if Atlas didn't show up, our chances looked slim. If he did? They were next to zero. There was no way we could successfully defend the city. And why wouldn't he show up? What would stop him from coming here to finish what he couldn't on the steps in Washington? Definitely not one of us.

"Well, then, we'll die defending this city," I said.

They all turned to look at me. "You can't be serious," Doug said.

I nodded. "Everybody's looking at us, seeing what we'll do. People are counting on us. Depending on us. We have to show them that we won't give up. We'll fight until our dying breath, and then we'll be martyrs. We can't inspire people to give up. We have to inspire them to fight. Our only option is to fight. Whether or not we're fighting to win, that's up to you."

Nobody would look me or anybody else in the eye. Their gazes wandered around the room as they considered what I'd said.

Selena sighed. "He's right," she said, looking at everybody.

"We really don't have a choice. We can't run and hide. We have to show everybody that we're not going to give up. But I disagree with you on one part of that, Kane," she said, turning to me. "This isn't going to be a final battle. We're not going to die today. We're going to fight, and we're going to win. We're going to defend this city."

"She's right," Samantha said as she nodded. She turned to me, smiling. "This isn't a final battle. This is the beginning of a war."

Chapter 52
The Siege of Dallas

THE SOLDIERS OF the Legion of Richter were marching alongside their tanks as they entered Dallas. I looked to my right, where Selena was floating next to me, decked out in her Holocene gear.

I pulled up the hood of my fresh Tempest outfit. "You ready?" I asked.

She nodded. "Let's get this party started."

I grinned, and we moved into action. I flew fast and hard, straight for the tank at the front of the line of ten. I grabbed its barrel as I flew over and peeled it back like the lid on a can of food. It flew over my head and I brought it down like a hammer onto the tank in front of me. The tank folded in on itself, destroyed.

The multitude of soldiers around me began to realize what was going on. I jumped out of the way an instant before they began firing their weapons at me. Some fired bolts of Eximus, while others fired regular bullets.

I flew back toward Holocene, who was holding Hank in her hands. I grabbed his ankles, while she had hold of his wrists. We stretched him out twenty feet and flew down the line of soldiers to the right of the tanks, knocking them off their feet. We flew down until we reached the forth tank, then flew up and out of the way as the other soldiers began to figure out what was happening and got their guns ready to fire.

I let go of Hank and he came back to his regular self. Holocene flew off with him, and I looked at the damage we'd done so far. Two tanks and a hundred or so soldiers.

Eight tanks and twenty-four hundred more soldiers to go.

Two Supers spotted me and flew up from the rear of the soldiers, coming right for me.

"Two Supers, headed my way," I said to Samantha.

"Relaying the message," she replied.

I turned around and flew away. They were going to have to chase me.

I flew toward downtown, the Supers hot on my tail. I flew fast enough that they couldn't catch me, but slow enough that they thought they could. I barreled straight for one of the skyscrapers, showing no signs of wavering. To them, it looked like I'd go right through the building.

Right before I hit it, I changed my flight path, flying straight up. I heard a crashing sound behind me and looked over my shoulder. One of them hadn't turned in time and had gone straight through the building. The other had been able to turn, though, and was right on my tail. His blond hair whipped in the wind, and his face showed his determination to take me down.

I reached the top of the building and crested over it. I began flying straight down toward the ground. If the Super who had gone through the building had slowed down a bit upon impact, that meant he should reappear out the other side just in time.

The Super shot out the side of the building in an explosion

of glass, right in front of me. I slammed into him, causing him to let out a grunt of surprise. I kept hold of him as I rocketed toward the ground. He was in so much shock that I'd grabbed him that he didn't have time to fight back.

I threw him at the ground just before I reached it. I changed my path before I too hit the ground and flew straight down the street, just inches from the pavement.

When I looked behind me I saw the one I'd thrown wasn't getting up from his crater in the pavement. The blond guy was hot on my tail, though. Glass from cars and buildings exploded all around us as we flew lighting fast down the street.

"Tell Drew to be ready! I'm leading this guy up!" I shouted to Samantha.

"Got it! He and Nep are ready for you."

I shot to the right once I'd reached the end of the street, my stomach almost touching the sides of the buildings as I flew diagonally toward the sky. I flew toward a skyscraper that had a large gap near the top of it. As I flew toward it, for some reason I thought about an episode of the TV show *Dallas* where they'd flown a helicopter through the gap. Well, now they were about to add two superhumans to the list of things flown through the skyscraper's gap.

I flew directly toward it, picking up the pace a little bit. The Super following me could clearly see where I was headed, so I wanted to make the space between us a bit larger. Wouldn't want to get caught up in Drew's trap.

I reached the gap, flying straight through it. The Super was right behind me, but he didn't see that Nep was hiding above the gap, Drew in hand. Nep fell in line behind my pursuer, unbeknownst to him. I looked over my shoulder and watched as Nep closed in on him, holding Drew by the bulletproof vest he was wearing. Drew gave a single tap to the Super and his powers were zapped from him. He fell toward the ground, hit the top of a building and went right through the roof. He presumably fell through six stories before he hit the ground. He'd be out of commission for a while. These Supers weren't nearly as powerful as I was, so their regeneration powers didn't work nearly as quickly as mine—if they even had them at all. Their not having those powers was definitely a possibility, but that was a gamble I was willing to take.

"Where's Selena?" I asked Samantha.

An explosion sounded behind me. The tanks were beginning to fire into the city, destroying buildings.

"She's trying to take out some of the tan—shit! She just got hit by an E-bolt!" Samantha shouted.

It took me a split second to realize Samantha was referring to an Eximus bolt. I did a zero degree turn, flying toward the tanks and soldiers. I had to get Selena out of there before they pounced on her.

I flew over the tanks—which were now rolling down the interstate overpass in a horizontal formation—and saw Selena lying on top of one of them. Soldiers were climbing up on top of them to retrieve her.

I swooped down as one of them reached for her. I grabbed her, pulling her in to my chest.

This time, they were ready for me. A barrage of E-bolts flew through the air, right for me. Two of them made contact, and I went fell toward the ground. Using what human power I had in me, I turned my back to the ground, protecting Selena. Then I soared over the edge of the overpass and felt my powers returning as I hit the road, sliding across it.

I came to a stop and felt my body begin to repair itself.

Selena put a hand on my chest and pushed off, rising to her feet. She reached her hand down, and I grabbed it. She pulled me up. "Thanks, but that makes us nowhere near even."

"Yeah, you've saved my ass more than a few times," I said. I looked over Selena's shoulder and saw soldiers beginning to run down the slopes on the sides of the overpass. "Shit," I said.

Selena turned, and the two of us were ready to begin taking care of the soldiers.

A gunshot rang out behind me and one of the Legion soldiers went down. I turned around and saw a man in his forties standing there, rifle in hand. Behind him, more people began to appear, each of them carrying their own weapons and ammunition. Some of them were police officers, while others were dressed in army fatigues. Most of them were regular citizens, however. There were about thirty or forty of them in all.

"You take care of those tanks. We've got this," the man who'd shot first said.

They all ran to find cover as a firefight between them and the soldiers began to break out.

Selena and I flew up out of their way.

"There's a handful of them, and over two thousands soldiers marching down the interstate. They'll be dead in a heartbeat," Samantha said.

"They're not taking on the entire army, just the stragglers trying to get into downtown right here," I said. "This is what we hoped for. We're inspiring people to fight with us." I couldn't help but smile. This was actually working. We were actually going to win this battle.

"Kane, Nep says there's another line of soldiers and tanks coming in from a different part of the city," Samantha said.

That smile left my face.

Chapter 53
Reinforcements

SELENA AND I flew to Nep, who was waiting for us on the west side of downtown.

"It looks like there's as many over here as there is back with you guys," he said, pointing down at them.

Nep was right. There were just as many of them. Explosions sounded back in the direction we'd just come from.

"They're starting to do some real damage to the city," Selena said. "We need to think of something, quick."

I began to think, hard and fast. We needed something big. Something spectacular. Something that'd scare them. But something was missing. There was no clear target for us to take out.

"Who's their leader?" I thought aloud.

Selena looked at me, realization dawning on her. "You're right. They have no clear leader. But somebody has to be calling the shots."

I nodded. "If we can find out who it is, we can take them down. No leader, and they'll fall apart. They won't know what to do."

I looked back down at this new faction of soldiers, and

something caught my eye. Someone was riding in a large Humvee at the back of the line. I looked closely and saw that sitting in the passenger seat of the vehicle was Sven. I pointed toward him, Selena and Nep following my gaze. "I think our teleporter friend got himself a promotion."

Selena scoffed. "That son of a bitch."

"We can't do it where both factions of soldiers will see, though. We'll take him out in front of this group. That should be enough to make them retreat," I said.

"What about the other group?" Nep asked.

I smirked. "I've got an idea for them." I turned to Selena. "I'll get him out of the vehicle. You do the rest."

Selena nodded.

"Nep, you go make sure those people fighting for us stay safe."

"Will do. Good luck," he said as he flew off.

"Alright, get ready. This'll happen fast," I told Selena.

I flew down toward the group of soldiers. I spotted one who had an Eximus gun and yanked it from him. Then I headed straight for Sven's Humvee. He didn't see me coming at all. I fired two blasts into his vehicle. One shattered the windshield, the other took out his ability to teleport.

He convulsed in his seat, unable to escape. I landed on the hood of his vehicle and ripped the roof off, then pulled off his seatbelt and yanked him from his seat. I flew fast toward the front of the line of soldiers and brought him to his knees twenty feet in front of them. Then I fired another blast into him, making sure his powers wouldn't be coming back anytime soon.

"Everybody, look here!" I shouted.

Soldiers raised their guns, but didn't fire. They didn't know what I was going to do to their leader.

"You will turn around. You will retreat. We will show you no mercy."

Selena swooped in and grabbed the barrel of one of the tanks. She was doing the same hammer maneuver I'd done earlier; she began to swing the barrel over her shoulder like it was nothing.

I fired one last bolt into Sven and jumped out of the way, hovering over the scene.

Holocene brought the tank down onto Sven as hard as she could.

The soldiers stood there for a beat, taking in what had just happened.

A blast shot from the next tank in line, directly at me. I dodged out of the way and it flew right into an apartment complex, blowing a hole that stretched from the seventh to the ninth floor.

Holocene got out of there and joined me, and the two of us flew to safety. The soldiers with Eximus guns began firing their weapons in every direction. They were making sure we didn't come close to them again as they continued their assault on Dallas.

I thought back to those two Supers that I'd taken out earlier. Of course. They were the leaders of that other faction of Supers, and my taking them out had done nothing to slow them down. I couldn't believe I didn't think about that.

"What are we going to do?" Selena asked, looking down at the thousands of people who were marching on her city, now protected by shooting off their E-bolts.

"I don't know," I said. "We can't even get close." Then I

remembered my idea for the other faction of soldiers. "But I don't think we'll need to."

"What do you mean?" Selena asked.

"You focus on that other faction. Do whatever you can to take them out. Any means necessary. We can't hold back anymore."

She nodded. We'd intended to do this with as few casualties as possible, but that wasn't a possibility anymore. They needed to know that we meant business.

"Are you sure you can take this faction out on your own?" Selena asked.

"I've got this."

Selena and I went our separate ways. She went to join Nep. I had faith that the two of them would figure something out.

I smiled as I thought of my plan. This was definitely something they weren't going to see coming.

I flew toward the famed Reunion Tower. It was the large building in the Dallas skyline, with a top that looked like a Christmas ornament. It was a large ball that would light up at night, sometimes in different colors, depending on the occasion. On the inside were restaurants, observatory decks, and all sorts of little shops. Today, it would be used to end this battle.

I flew beneath the large ball and gave its support one hard punch. That was all it took; the ball began to roll forward and fall toward the ground. I flew beneath it and pushed up on it. Even for someone as strong as I was, this thing was heavy. Very heavy. I let out a shout as I pushed up on it as hard as I could without flying straight through it. The ball continued to fall toward the ground, but it began to slow. I strained harder and harder until finally it stopped falling just a few feet from the ground.

Now came lifting it. Since I didn't have the momentum of it falling working against me, lifting was much easier. I flew upward, holding the top of the Reunion Tower above my head. I picked up speed as I flew toward the faction of soldiers, who were still firing their Eximus guns into the air. They'd be useless against the Reunion Tower.

I came closer and closer, picking up speed.

"Kane, are you sure you want to do this?" Samantha asked.

"Yes, I'm sure."

"Once we do this, we can't go back."

"Now's not the time, Samantha."

"Some of these people are just fighting because they're afraid of what will happen to them if they don't."

"What else are we supposed to do? They're going to kill everyone they can to take back this city." I picked up more speed. I was getting closer and closer to my target.

"There has to be another way, Kane."

"We don't have time for another way, Samantha. This is war."

I pushed on the ball in my hands, launching it at the faction of soldiers. It slammed into them, the E-bolts hitting it doing nothing.

One faction down, one to go.

Chapter 54
Just the Beginning

JUST A FEW minutes after I brought the Reunion Tower down on my faction of soldiers, the first faction was in retreat.

"Everybody, meet back at the office. I think it's over," Samantha said in my mind.

I flew back to the office feeling numb. I couldn't believe it was over, but I was beginning to regret what I'd done to ensure our victory. It was a decision made in the heat of battle, and had I given it more thought, I might've been able to come up with something else. But they were getting closer and closer to a city with over a million people. People who'd seen the Legion kill the president on TV just a few hours earlier.

A million versus a few thousand. And the few thousand would've won. That was the power of fear.

I reached the office building the same time as Holocene and Nep did, carrying Hank and Drew respectively.

"Is that it?" Drew asked, a big smile on his face. "Is this really over?"

I looked at everyone's faces, and they all seemed happy. Satisfied. All of them but Samantha.

“I think so,” Nep said with a laugh. He and Drew high-fived. The celebration spread as everybody began patting each other on the back, congratulating themselves on a job well done.

“There’s no going back,” Samantha said in my head, the two of us staring at each other from across the room as everybody else celebrated around us.

“I did what I had to,” I said, barely above a whisper.

Samantha gave me a sad smile. “If that’s what you think, then okay. I’ll respect your decision. I don’t support it.”

I nodded, accepting her compromise.

“That was too easy,” Hank said.

Everybody turned and looked at him.

“What do you mean?” I asked.

He shrugged as he tried to think of a good reason. “I don’t know. It was just…you know…too easy. Something was wrong. Is wrong. I can just…feel it.”

Hank’s words caused an ominous atmosphere to set in. My brain began to fire as I tried to think of what he could mean by that. It hadn’t seemed easy to me, but then again Hank hadn’t played that big of a role. He didn’t have my perspective, or Selena’s.

“Oh shit. Holy shit. Shit shit shit,” Doug said, slamming his fist on his desk.

“What is it?” Samantha shouted.

Everybody ran to Doug, who pointed at his computer screen. “This was all just a distraction. It was too easy because they weren’t even trying.”

I looked at his computer screen and was so taken aback by what I saw there that I actually fell to the floor. I couldn’t believe what I was seeing. This was actually happening. My mind raced, and I thought I was going to puke. I did, a little. I swallowed it down and gasped for air. I was having a panic attack, wasn't I? That's what it felt like. My whole body shook. So much energy rushed through me, I wanted to run and run and fly and run and never stop.

It was true. This was real. It was all real. We had fallen for Atlas' distraction. He'd played us beautifully.

I read the screen one last time before closing my eyes and crying.

HOURS AFTER DEATH OF PRESIDENT, TWO NUKES SET OFF IN NEW YORK CITY AND LOS ANGELES. MILLIONS DEAD. LEGION OF RICHTER CLAIMING RESPONSIBILITY.

CHAPTER 55
ULTIMATUM

I TOOK A DEEP breath. I always got nervous in front of cameras.

"You ready for this?" Samantha said, her finger on the record button.

I nodded.

"Rolling," she said.

Doug clicked a button on his recorder. "Speed."

Drew was holding the boom pole, a microphone attached to the end of it.

"Whenever you're ready," Samantha said. "You'll do fine," she added in my head.

I smiled at her and took one more deep breath.

"Hello. My name is Kane Andrews, also known as the superhero Tempest. As you may know, Atlas and his Legion of Richter have taken many millions of lives. He and his people think that they can take over, ruling with fear and anarchy. They think they can do whatever they want, and can kill whoever stands in their way. I'm here to tell you that they can't. I'm here to tell you that they're wrong. My name is Kane Andrews, and I am not alone. I'm here to tell you that there is no reason to be afraid. We will fight back against Atlas. We will win. They will not destroy us.

"If you stand with me, we can destroy Atlas and the Legion of Richter. I've killed Richter once, and I can kill him again. This time, I need your help. If you want to join the fight against Atlas, come to Dallas, Texas. Dallas is a safe haven for all. No one will be turned away, and we will protect the city at all costs.

"And to Atlas, who I know is watching this, be afraid. This will not be as easy as you thought. We will not go down without a fight.

"My name is Kane Andrews, also known as the superhero Tempest. This is my ultimatum."

Chapter 56

Down but Not Out

LOREN COULDN'T BELIEVE the events of the day. She was lying on the couch in her office inside the top-secret STF underground base. Her new home, really. No way was it safe enough to go back to her apartment in Washington. Besides, she had too much work to do.

There was a knock at the door. "Come in," she said as she sat up on her couch.

The door opened and in walked Agent Wells, her new right hand after York's death in the attack on the STF compound. "Just letting you know that this base is now officially under STF command. We've put up the new logo on everything," he said with a smile as he rubbed his hand over his slicked-back hair, making sure everything stayed in its place.

Director Loren smiled and nodded. "Good. Thank you."

This was now officially her domain. It had once been used by the CIA, but they had transferred all power and resources to the STF. In a way, Loren was now the most powerful human on the planet. She had all the resources she needed to figure out a way to destroy the Supers once and for all.

"What's our next move, ma'am?" Agent Wells asked.

Loren smirked and chuckled as she thought of it. "Right now, Wells, take the rest of the day off."

Agent Wells looked at her, confused. "I'm sorry, ma'am. I don't understand."

"This base isn't fully operational yet. We're still bringing our people in from the field. It'll be another day or two before the real work begins. Until then, get some rest. You're going to need it."

Agent Wells smiled and began backing out of the room. "Of course, ma'am. You're right. I'll talk to you in the morning, then. If you need anything, just let me know."

"I will," Loren said.

Agent Wells exited the room, shutting the door behind him.

Loren was once again alone in her new office. She would get some rest too. As much as she could get. Because once her new STF base was running at maximum capacity, she would get no sleep at all. She'd be working 24/7, deep underground, until she was ready. All the while the Supers would be fighting above her in their trivial war, weakening each other. She would hide away, biding her time, and once they were weak—she'd strike. Finishing them all for good.

Loren lay back down on her couch and closed her eyes with a smile on her face. She would sleep well. Perhaps her best sleep ever, because she'd sleep knowing that it wouldn't be long before her plan was set in motion. It wouldn't be long until all the Supers were eradicated, now and forever.

Director Loren of the Super Task Force fell asleep as a human for the last time.

About the Author

Logan Rutherford is a twenty year old author living in Los Angeles. He writes full time, and loves hearing from his readers. You can get in contact with him at the following places:

www.authorloganrutherford.com
@loganrutherford
facebook.com/loganwrites
authorloganrutherford@gmail.com

Thank you for reading.